Dear Kieren,

So proud of you honey.
I hope you enjoy the
read.

Lots of love

Aunty Anita

AK Sharma
10.4.2021

AK SHARMA

The Twelve Keys

europe books

www.europebooks.co.uk

ISBN 979-12-201-0406-7
First edition: December 2020

The Twelve Keys

With a desire and a flicker of hope that magic could really exist,
That Santa Claus, Papa Noel and Father Christmas is the real deal.
That animals do sometimes think and behave like humans and vice-versa,
that perhaps a fantasy world can and does exist somewhere in our Universe.

To all those who want to lose themselves in another world for a short time,
I hope you enjoy the magical fantasy that is the 'Kingdom of Shengxiao'.

To all you non-believers, read it and perhaps you will want to believe…

Dedicated!

Contents

The unicorns were the most recognizable magic the fairies possessed, and they sent them to those worlds where belief in the magic was in danger of falling altogether. After all there has to be some belief in magic- however small- for any world to survive.

Terry Brooks

CHAPTER ONE

Wyetta held the sword in her hand turning it slowly as it gleamed brightly in the sunlight. "Finally, it was finished", sighed Wyetta, it had taken her many weeks to make it and now it was done. The dream about the sword had come to her as she slept. Night after night it had whirled through her mind, waking her at the same point within the dream, when the face of the Dragongold was to be revealed. "Who was the Dragongold?", whispered Wyetta shaking her head in frustration as the image never materialised.

Wyetta did not know how the two were connected, but she did know that it had something to do with the Dragon Games. This is what puzzled her most. The Dragon Games had been banned hundreds of years ago by the Gods who had replaced them with the Shengxiao Games. Gaining one of the Twelve Keys to the Heavenly Gates was the ultimate prize in the Kingdom of Shengxiao, and through the Games was the only way to attain one.

Wyetta looked at the etchings engraved on the blade of the Five Earthly Elements, Water, Earth, Metal, Fire and Wood. That had been most difficult to do as she had to make sure that the etchings *'lived'* within the sword. The magic was new to her, it was incredibly old magic, and it had cost her dearly. Wyetta gazed across at her reflection in the mirror hanging on the wall on the far side of the room barely recognizing herself.

The magic to make the sword had aged her, her beautiful long dark hair had changed, white hair having weaved its way through giving her the appearance of someone much older.

Wyetta looked at the blade again tracing her fingers softly over the etchings. As her fingers touched the etching of the Water Element, it started to change becoming liquid in form. It rippled across the blade changing it completely. Wyetta touched the tip of the blade to the floor watching mesmerised as a puddle started to form. It was only when the water started to creep towards her bare feet, did she lift the tip of the floor squeezing the hilt as she did so. Only when the sword had transformed back to its' original form did Wyetta loosen her grip. It was indeed a special sword destined for someone who would play a major role in her life, she was sure of that.

Wyetta took one last look at the sword before she moved towards a long tapestry on the wall. Pulling it to one side, a small wooden door was revealed. She muttered something under her breath causing the door to swing open leading to a long dark corridor. Wyetta entered closing the door quietly behind her. She would hide the sword until such time it was needed. Who it belonged to? she did not know. The spell cast ensured that only the person to whom the sword belonged would be able to reveal its whereabouts. As Wyetta finished her spell she uttered the word "Vanish".

Taking one last look at the small "empty" chamber she walked out of the door.

"Rebel, Rebel, we need you to come quickly to the home of the Ratticus High Elders something terrible has happened", Drizzle had used mind-meld to get hold of Rebel. It was a unique skill he shared with his twin brother Crick.

"Whaat, Drizzle do you know it's the middle of the night?", responded Rebel with a wide yawn still half asleep.

"Rebel do not delay, I fear for the safety of the High Elders, please come quickly", this time as well as Drizzle, Crick, his twin brother had also entered his mind. Rebel could feel an impending sense of doom coming from them both. "This was not good", he thought to himself as he got up from his bed, quickly pulling on his clothes. "Okay, I'm on my way Drizzle, send a message to Storm and ask him to meet me there", finished Rebel as he left his room.

Rebel swiftly made his way through the moonlit streets of the Kingdom. He hoped it was nothing serious as the annual Shengxiao Games were due to take place the following week and he was looking forward to having a quiet week to prepare for the Games. The Games were due to take place on the rising of the Pink Moon, which was always on the fourth month of the year. Many years ago, the Games had been started by the Gods for the citizens of the Kingdom of Shengxiao. The prize being one of the coveted Twelve Keys to the Heavenly Gates.

The Games were now just played for fun for all to enjoy as an annual get together, as the same families had held their Keys since the Games began.

Rebel loved taking part in the Games with his friends and was looking forward to them this year too. He looked up at the moon as he ran through the streets, it was nearly a full moon just a week to go he thought to himself.

It took him nearly twenty minutes to reach the area of the Kingdom called the Colony, home of the Ratticus Clan. As Rebel approached the Hole of the High Elders, Storm joined him silently from the shadows. Rebel nodded briefly at him as they approached the entrance to the High Elders' Hole where Drizzle and Crick were waiting for them, both looking very agitated.

"Rebel we fear they have been killed", Crick whispered quietly, "they have not been seen for a few days, so we came to check on them. We have not entered their Hole, the smell coming from there is very unpleasant". Storm went closer to the entrance and sniffed deeply, "You are right Crick, that is the smell of death", Storm looked at Rebel as he spoke matter-of-factly with his nose wrinkled distastefully.

"Do you have a key to open the door Drizzle?", Rebel asked. Drizzle shook his head, "No Rebel, but we know how to get in without the key", responded Drizzle indicating to his brother Crick to climb the wall and enter the house via the secret entrance that was a common feature in all the Holes of the Colony. Crick quickly transformed into his animal, before scuttling up the wall. Rebel watched as Crick disappeared out of sight, his long tail giving a quick flick back as it too vanished.

Before long Rebel heard a bolt being scraped back, the main door to the Hole opened slowly revealing Crick, now back in human form, his hand held over his nose. The smell wafting out was nauseating, both Storm and Rebel covered their noses quickly before entering.

"Drizzle you guard the door", Rebel instructed his voice muffled by his hand.

The smell became even more unbearable as they made their way downwards deeper into the Hole to the main part of the High Elders home. As they entered the main chamber, they could see High Elder Jed lying on the floor, his lifeless arm was thrown over his wife, Zelda, in a protective gesture, both were most definitely dead. Crick gave a strangled cry unable to contain himself as he knelt next to the bodies, "Who could have done this Rebel? Why would they want to kill the High Elders of the Ratticus?"

"The Key!", Storm and Rebel exclaimed at the same time. The Twelve Keys were coveted by each of the twelve families. All the families made sure that every year they kept their Key by winning the challenges set for each family. Never had anything like this happened before, the death of the Ratticus High Elders meant that their Key had now become available for any family who did not hold a key, to challenge in the Games.

Drizzle came running in looking extremely distraught, "How? Why? Who did this?", he exclaimed.

"I thought I told you to guard the door", Rebel gave Crick a cross look, "I couldn't help it, we're twins we know what each is thinking", mumbled Crick looking at Drizzle then Rebel despondently.

"Okay now that you are here, all of you search for any clues as to what may have happened. I must go to the palace and inform King Varick of the situation", with a brief backward glance at the two bodies, Rebel left to make his way quickly back to the Palace.

"Come on we have to go now otherwise we'll miss everything", shouted Mercy. It was the night of the Shengxiao Games, the moon would be bigger and brighter than any other night turning a shade of pink rarely seen. Many people in the Kingdom saw this as an auspicious time, so all were heading out to enjoy the festivities on the highest point of the Kingdom, Boundary Hill which was situated only a short distance from Sheng Forrest.

With the murder of the High Elders of the Ratticus Family the excitement of the Games had been dulled thought Rebel. All knew that the potential for the Key to be won by another family other than the Ratticus would cause major challenges to the King and the other eleven families.

The Games were due to start in a few hours, King Varick and Queen Althea were to present the Key to the Heavenly Gate to the new High Elders at dawn. Nobody knew what form the Key would take as each family were given a different key to protect the Gates. The secret of the Keys had always been held by the reigning King, only King Varick and the Key holder would know the secret.

King Varick and Queen Althea were part of the Ledary Clan of the Dragonion Family, home was Druk Yul the capital city of the Kingdom. King Varick was a strong King, much loved by the citizens of Shengxiao. He was majestic and fearsome at the same time, dressed tonight in his traditional colours of Royal Red and Gold. Circling his head was a Crown created from gold only found in Adraga the coastal city of the Thunder Dragons and protectors of the magical Caysand.

Queen Althea was famed for her breath-taking beauty, with green eyes and long flame-coloured tresses, held together by gold and diamond chains which linked to the Gold and Diamond Circlet on her head. Althea was dressed in a gown of emerald green, with diamonds detailed into the fabric of the dress, that shone brightly in the moonlight causing them to sparkle, resembling thousands of tiny stars.

Varick and Althea had borne triplets, which was rare for Dragonians. As was natural in the Dragonian Clan their offspring had been blessed with magical powers which were unique to each of them.

The oldest of the three was Princess Sofia, she had been blessed with the knowledge of her ancestors. This gift allowed Sofia to recall all that had occurred in the history of the Dragonian Clan.

The knowledge Sofia held was invaluable to King Varick, so he had given the responsibility of the People's Library to Princess Sofia. Sofia was quiet by nature, spending a lot of her time reading books on the Magic of the Druk which also helped her to understand better the knowledge she recalled.

Princess Sofia had inherited her father's dark hair and brown eyes resembling him more than her two brothers. Due to be married in the next year Sofia was busy preparing for her wedding to Dragonian High Lord Sylvest. Lord Sylvest came from a very influential family and would make a good match for Princess Sofia, so her father had blessed the union.

Prince Raulf was born one minute later with Prince Jai nearly ten minutes after his siblings.

Of the three Prince Jai was the more popular within the Kingdom, making friends everywhere he went. Jai was tall, at least a head taller than Raulf, with a thick dark mane of hair which was tied back with a leather thong, the current fashion in Druk.

With strong facial bone structure and a body that was lithe and athletic, he was immensely popular with the girls. Jai's distinguishing feature were his eyes, dark brown with flecks of gold they reflected his warmth and inner strength. His looks were neither that of his father nor of his mother but inherited from his forefathers.

Jai was special in that he, out of all the royal family resembled the Dragonian Clan most as his features showed more of his inner self than the others. This was his magic gift as it allowed him to transform his aura into dragon within a split second, as well as the ability, to transform back to his human form just as fast.

Looking nothing like his siblings, Raulf had inherited his mother's flaming red hair and green eyes. The King had on many occasions expressed his concern to Rebel regarding Raulf's special gift, one that had not been seen for an exceptionally long time within the Dragonians. Rebel did not know what the gift entailed except that it was a rare Blue Aura. He had been tasked along with Sophia to research what the blue aura signified, yet, neither Rebel nor Sophia had had much luck.

Concerned Varick had asked Rebel to keep an eye on Prince Raulf discreetly. Not sure why, Rebel did as he was bid. Over the few months that he had been watching Raulf, Rebel began to realise that the unrest in the City was being caused by Raulf.

The more Rebel listened to the chatter, the more concerned he became, especially since the murder of the Ratticus Elders had still not been solved. This eve Rebel had a specific job to do at the games and it would involve all his team to ensure that the Games went smoothly.

All three siblings were seated around their parents, drinking and eating whilst waiting for the games to begin. Bells would be rung to signify the start of the games and everyone was waiting in anticipation for that moment.

Traditionally in the past, the Games were supposed to involve all the Twelve Families in the Kingdom, over the years this had changed to only the families who were choosing High Elders. However, King Varick had announced that this time the games would be run as they were meant, to that end, all the families of the Kingdom had been informed to be prepared.

Rebel quickly pulled out of his magical trance and reverie, just as he was shifting his vision back to where the Royal Family sat, by Mercy shouting very loudly.

"Rebel, Storm, Drizzle, Crick, hurry up I want to see everything and not miss anything". Mercy was the only female of the group and belonged to the Panthera Family. Like all the Panthera she was unbelievably beautiful. Unknown to Rebel she was also desperately in love with him.

"We're coming", Rebel shouted, at the same time he ushered Storm, Drizzle and Crick out of the front door. "Come on boys let's go you know Mercy will be mad if we don't get there on time" he shouted as he vaulted out of the door behind them.

"But the first few hours are so boring", grumbled Storm as they made their way down the street. Storm was the lazy one in the group he would rather just eat, sleep and do nothing else unless forced to. Storm belonged to the Felinia Clowder with green eyes that glowed at night he had a skin colour that was as dark as the night sky. Nobody really knew how he had become one of their 'gang' as the Felinia Clowder lived on the outskirts of the Kingdom and those who lived there rarely came to the City of Druk Yul.

Storm had become a much-loved part of the group as he had got into the habit of resolving any fights or arguments between them. Unknown to many, he was also Rebel's right hand.

Storm had skills that allowed him, despite his size, to climb anything quickly. Along with this special ability he was resourceful and cunning which was a huge asset to Rebel. Storm and Rebel normally worked together, although outward appearances showed otherwise.

Rebel looked sideways at him now and grinned, "You know you love it when we go early as there's going to be so much food, you will be fit to burst by the morning with everything you will eat", he said as they jogged quickly after Mercy and the others, following them down the high street and out of the city gates towards Boundary Hill.

The night was calm and the breeze warm for this time of year. With the sky clear of any clouds the moon shone brightly above them lighting the road to Boundary hill. Ahead of them they could see many people walking towards the 'Mound' as it was more fondly known.

Rebel could see families he had known all his life walking ahead of him, all dressed for the occasion. As they walked quickly towards the Mound, Rebel saw the blacksmiths son, Keon, who was part of the Oxbow Herd. The Oxbow inhabited the Grasslands which formed the boundaries of the Kingdom, it was here where all the food for the Kingdom was grown.

Keon was walking alongside his betrothed Beda, who was one of the Warrior Maids to Queen Althea. 'Keon', Rebel shouted, both Beda and Keon turned when they heard his shout, giving a wave of acknowledgement they stopped walking, waiting for Rebel and his friends to catch up.

Keon was sturdily built, his arms strong with all the daily forging he did. He had short hair cropped to his scalp so all you could see was a shadow of his blond hair, with his face browned by the sun you could see the lighter shade of the laughter crinkles at the corner of his eyes that had deepened over the years, showing his fun-loving nature.

Beda on the other hand was slim, athletic and strong as was required in her role as the Head of the Warrior Maids. Beda was taller than Keon by a few inches with jet black hair and eyes to match. Her skin tone was nut brown in colour which glistened in the moonlight with the oil that been smoothed over it.

Beda also belonged to the Oxbow her parents being the High Elders of the Herd which was a great responsibility as the Oxbow were the providers of the Kingdoms' harvest every year.

Beda had been selected as Head of the Warrior Maids

only last year, it was the highest honour for Beda, who had worked hard to achieve this coveted position.

“Hey Rebel, you ready to be beaten in the games”, Keon said in jest. Keon knew that Rebel never lost. Rebel’s parentage was part Panthera and part Dragonian. He was renowned throughout the Kingdom as King Varick’s champion even though he still had to reach his Eighteenth birth year.

Rebel had developed many skills under the influence of King Varick. These skills were invaluable to Varick in maintaining peace in the Kingdom. Tonight, of all nights Rebel would be needed to keep the peace, especially with all the different High Elders and their families attending this special occasion.

“You can try Keon as always you will lose the bet and I’ll end up kissing Beda again as part of the bet”, laughed Rebel as they joked and walked towards the Mound. All the while Rebel was keeping an eye on what was going on around him, his keen senses inherited from his parents were on high alert.

“Not on your life Rebel”, said Beda as she shoved at him playfully. Beda was dressed in her Warrior Maid outfit of black and silver a clear indication of her position in the Royal household, with a gold band crowning her dark glossy hair marking her as the leader of the Warrior Maids. It was this role that meant Beda would be working tonight, making her way towards Queen Althea, where she would stay until the festivities were over.

The atmosphere was electric, families from all over the

Kingdom had come tonight to take part in the Games. After the games for the 'Choosing of the High Elders', for the Ratticus Family, the main games would begin, and they were going to be the highlight of the evening as the challenges, although a lot of fun, were also taken very seriously by all who took part.

Rebel had been appointed by King Varick as his personal advisor two years ago, when Rebel had foiled a plot against Queen Althea saving her life. Unknown to Rebel, King Varick was his uncle, Rebel's father was brother to King Varick, and a Dragonian. His father had married a Panthera Princess against the wishes of his family, for this he was outcast by the Ruling Elders of the Dragonian, against the wishes of his brother The King.

Varick's brother Tarrin, had contacted him when Rebel was in his Fourteenth Birthyear. The note he had sent to Varick, told him that Rebel had started to show skills and magic that were so far advanced, that he Tarrin, did not have the ability or knowledge to help his son.

At his brother's request Varick had sought out Rebel late in his Fifteenth Birthyear bringing him under his wing at the Palace. Nobody knew who Rebel was and Varick kept it that way as he personally undertook the task of shaping Rebel's special skills. The more Rebel learnt to master these skills the more dangerous he became to the enemies of the Kingdom.

Over the two years under Varick's tutelage Rebel had learnt that he indeed was 'special' with the skills he had inherited. From his Dragonian father he had magical ability, powerful physical strength, and a knowledge of his ancestors that surpassed even

Varick's own ability to recall. The last was a skill that he shared with Princess Sofia and one that Varick encouraged both to develop by working together. Rare in the Dragonian clan was the power of healing, which Rebel had also inherited, much to the King's surprise and delight when it had been discovered by chance during one of their training sessions when Varick had been badly hurt.

From his mother a Panthera, Rebel inherited the traits of determination, confidence, and courage. Along with a keen sense of smell and the ability to move with stealth. All of which he displayed in his role as the King's Spy.

Rebel could see the Mound about a quarter of mile ahead framed by brightly lit lanterns dotted everywhere. He could also hear the music being played even at this distance. As they continued walking, there were so many people on the road, that it was becoming more and more difficult to navigate through them slowing them down to a near standstill in parts.

Rebel suddenly veered off to the left with the others following him quickly, as he started to walk towards the shadowy edge of Sheng Forest around a hundred yards from the road.

Sheng Forest belonged to the Kingdom of Shengxiao, it was reserved exclusively for the Royal Hunts which took place twice yearly at Equinox. When day and night became equal in time the forest was at its best for the Royal Hunt, what was hunted only those in the Hunt would know when the time came.

As they entered the forest, small light orbs appeared above and just in front of each of them. Rebel's friends looked towards him as they knew he was responsible for the orbs.

They were always amazed at his magical ability, all going silent at the sight of the orbs as they appeared. They walked slowly through the forest, with the orbs floating along at the same pace casting a soft glow around them.

The noise of the road faded behind them as the group slowly picked their way through the dense forest towards the Mound, only the sound of the night animals foraging in the dark with the odd growling sound made its way to the group.

They finally cleared the forest some fifteen minutes after they had entered. Ahead of them in the distance, they could see the Mound. It took another twenty minutes across a small meadow before they started the uphill climb to the top. Looking up Rebel could see the faint glow of the lights that had been strung along the perimeter at the top of the mound.

"Let's go I can't wait much longer to see what food there is", Storm grinned at all of them before starting to make his way quickly up the Mound.

The higher they got the clearer the moon became, it was magnificent, "It was going to be a wonderful night", thought Rebel to himself, as the silent friends started to follow Storm, picking up their pace as the festivities got closer. The top of the Mound was half a mile in diameter and flat as a pancake. It was perfect for the Annual Shengxiao Games.

As the group reached the top they stopped, taking in the sight before them. To the left of the group a large Dias had been erected and decorated in the Royal colours of gold and white. Sitting on what can only be described as golden sand were King Varick and Queen Althea.

The sand held magical properties which allowed any who had magic to enhance it further when in contact with it. It was this that allowed Varick and Althea to display their magical auras which created soft glows for nearly ten feet around them. Known as Caysand from the city of Adraga, it had been guarded by the Thunder Dragons for centuries. For in the wrong hands the Caysand could be extremely dangerous.

As they all took in the sight before them, they could see that to the left of Queen Althea were her Warrior Maids all dressed in their ceremonial Black and Silver. To the right of the King were the Royal Guard, identified by their black and red uniform. Chosen from the best warriors in the Kingdom it was near impossible to get past them.

Shifting his gaze Rebel looked towards the area marked off for the games. It took up the full length of the mound and was at least a third of the way across. It had been sectioned of by wooden fences inter-dispersed with magical orbs to light the whole area.

Directly opposite the Dias on the other side of the Mound, stalls and tables had been set with food and drink. Next to them the musicians had set themselves up with various musical instruments being played, multi-coloured lighting lit up the bustling area for all to see.

Already many people were dancing to the toe-tapping tunes that flowed across the mound. The aromas of all the different dishes being cooked wafted across to where they stood, making their mouths water and bellies grumble, in anticipation of the delicious food they would eat this night.

Rebel noticed that as soon as they had reached the top of the Mound, Beda had left the group making her way quickly towards Queen Althea, Rebel did the same with a quick nod to Storm he disappeared into the crowd to do what he did best.

Drizzle and Crick also left the group to make their way to where the games would take place. As part of the Ratticus Family they were supporting the favourites Durai and Fleta in their challenge to become High Elders.

The twins were identical in every way bar one. Drizzle had a line of three moles from the corner of his right eye down to his cheek. This was the only identifying mark between the two of them. The twins were inseparable, spending every waking moment they could together. Their uniqueness was their ability to communicate silently between themselves. They had the ability to be able to read the minds of others, which made them a strong ally to Durai and Fleta, and of course to Rebel.

As Drizzle and Crick made their way towards the games area, Mercy, Keon and Storm followed their noses by making their way towards the food stalls.

“Food, food give me food”, grumbled Storm as he made his way towards the other side of the Mound and away from the central games. Mercy and Keon looked at each other grinning at Storm knowing that Storm would stay by the food for the rest of the evening if he could.

There were all kinds of dishes provided by the different families attending the games, it was a feast fit for kings. Within minutes Storm had piled his plate high with meats, fruits, nuts and breads, when no more could fit on his plate he started to wend his way towards the tables to sit and eat. Mercy and Keon watched him as he passed the drinks stall grabbing the largest tankard of milk, he took a huge swig with some of it dripping down his chin.

Mercy and Keon smiled at that as they also started to fill their plates. “How come he only drinks milk?”, Keon asked puzzled, “As long as I have known him, I have only ever seen him drink milk. I don’t understand it especially when there are tankards of beer right next to the milk”, Keon finished shaking his head.

“Come-on Keon surely you must have realised by now that he is a Felinia Black. What else would he drink?”, Mercy laughed at him as he looked at her in amazement.

“I did not know that, I have never seen a Felinia Black so how would I?”, he finished in a small voice, shaking his head slowly at what he had just found out.

Plates filled they both grabbed a tankard of beer each before they headed back to the games. With a quick wave and shout to Storm they disappeared into the crowd eating and chatting with each other.

They made their way towards Drizzle and Crick, as they too planned to support Durai and Fleta in the challenge. As they walked towards them Mercy glimpsed Rebel in the crowd walking quickly in the opposite direction to them. Rebel was in a hurry as he moved with ease through the crowd, using his special abilities to slip through.

Mercy sensed immediately that something was wrong changing direction quickly to follow Rebel. “Keon make your way to Beda and the Queen, something is wrong", Mercy spoke urgently to Keon.

Keon looked at Mercy following her gaze towards Rebel, who by now was disappearing quickly into the crowd. Keon nodded to Mercy as he quickened his pace towards Beda and the Queen.

Mercy being Pantherian quickly made her way towards Rebel, placing her food and drink on a table she was passing. Mercy was soon at his side, matching his steps.

"What's wrong Rebel?", Mercy whispered quietly. Rebel responded by grabbing her arm and pulling them both behind a tent, "I have been informed of a plot against the Kingdom, Mercy, it's going to take place here at the games tonight", whispered Rebel just as quietly.

"The threat comes from the Felinia Clowder. The Felinia Clowder have always resented the Ratticus Family. It seems they want to send a message to everyone here at the games, that although they are not of the Twelve Chosen, they are still a force to be reckoned with, and they desperately want a Key.

"There are only a few ways to get a key, to depose or discredit a family in the eyes of the Gods or through the Shengxiao Games, and it seems the latter is going to be the method the Felinia Clowder are going to use", Rebel relayed this quickly to Mercy at the same time he was quickly and quietly guiding them through to the back of the Dias where the Royal Family were seated.

The Keys were special with only Twelve in existence. Made by the Gods as rewards to the first twelve families who won the games when the Shengxiao Games first took place. The Keys opened the Heavenly Gates to the Gods, once inside, it was fabled that there was unlimited wealth, both in gold and knowledge available only to the Twelve Chosen Families.

Many within the Felinia Clowder resented the fact that they were not one of the Twelve Chosen, they also did not have High Elders as the other families. This had created many factions within the Clowder, all competing against each other. It was becoming harder and harder to maintain order.

Head of the Felinia Clowder was Master Zi, a wise old man who was a scholar and a teacher of philosophy. Nobody really knew how old Zi was, he had always just been, with wispy snowy white hair covering his head and a wrinkly face, Zi was respected and feared at the same time. As well as being old he was also rare for a Felinia. Zi's left eye was blue, the other brown. Linked to this phenomenon of a blue eye was the fact that he was also deaf in his left ear.

This did not hinder Zi in any way in fact, it heightened all his other senses which he used to his advantage, making him a strong leader and a force to be reckoned with. Challenges for his position had taken place within the Clowder many times, all of them unsuccessful.

Within the Clowder was another faction, the Glaring. This was the group Zi had faced many challenges from in the past. It was this that was worrying Zi tonight. Zi had been informed a plot against the Ratticus Family with the sole intention of gaining their Key to the Heavenly Gate. Zi also knew, that the only way to gain one of the Twelve Keys, was to topple one of the families who held a Key, this would result in taking their place within the Kingdom and the Twelve Chosen.

Sadly, Zi was also keenly aware that the Felinia Clowder hated the Ratticus Family. It was going to be hard for him to convince the Glaring that this challenge would be futile.

The Ratticus Family were strong it would be foolish to try to challenge them today, the day of the Games and in front of all the other families. It could potentially mean the downfall of the Clowder so Zi had to stop this from happening, for the sake of his people. To this end and to maintain the peace he summoned the leader of the Glaring, Jonas, at the same time sending a messenger to find Rebel.

The sound of bells could be heard loud and clear across the mound, signifying the start of the Games. First would be the games to choose the High Elders for the Ratticus, after which the main games would begin.

As the crowd waited in heightened anticipation for the games to start, a lone figure wearing a black hooded cape which completely covered his head, walked towards the Dias and King Varick.

"HALT, WHO GOES THERE?", realising that it was not any of the contestants Beda shouted to the approaching figure. At the same time, she pulled out her short sword, signalling her Warrior Maids to follow suit. Conall Leader of the Kings Guard had been talking to one of his men when he heard Beda's shout. Realising very quickly something was seriously wrong, he jumped quickly onto the Dias to stand in front of the King, shielding him from the approaching figure.

The rest of the warriors quickly formed a semi-circle in

front of the Royal Family raising their weapons as they did so. The crowd which had been cheering loudly slowly went silent, shocked at what was unfolding before them.

"YOUR MAJESTY", the lone figure spoke loudly, "I WISH TO ANNOUNCE A CHALLENGE FOR A KEY TO THE HEAVENLY GATES", making sure that those closest to him in the crowd could hear what he said.

A murmuring started in the crowd with voices getting steadily louder, people asking each other what was being said and what was happening, as those further behind could not see or hear the caped figure.

"AND YOU ARE?", boomed King Varick as he leaned forward to take a closer look at the challenger.

"I am from the Felinia Clowder, Leader of the Glaring. I am within my rights to make this challenge as stated in the Book of the High Elders, anyone can make a challenge for a Key when a Key becomes available, AND I believe that a Key has become available" ... with that the cloaked figure threw back his hood revealing himself.

The crowd gasped at the sight of him, it was Jonas from the Glaring. Jonas was well known in the Kingdom as a nasty troublemaker and as such was much disliked by many of the families. Here he was making trouble of the worst kind Rebel thought as he watched from behind the Dias with Mercy at his side.

The King stood up and stared at him balefully, inwardly knowing that Jonas was right. A challenge for the Key could be made, this spelled trouble for all who were attending tonight, he thought to himself. It meant that all the Families had now been challenged unwittingly by Jonas, including his own for the right to hold a Key.

Thirteen families and only Twelve Keys!

The crowd had gone silent, not a whisper to be heard, Rebel had quietly come to stand just behind the King and whispered in his ear, "Your Majesty, I have received a message from Master Zi requesting a meeting, I think I know what about now. May I suggest that you delay the games for a short while to attend the meeting, as I believe Master Zi might be able to help with this situation", finished Rebel who was staring directly at Jonas.

King Varick, gave an imperceptible nod to Rebel, at the same time announcing to the crowd that a short delay would take place to consider the challenge, in the meantime he commanded, they should continue to enjoy the festivities. With that he turned around to face his family who by now had also stood up and were standing directly behind him.

"My Queen and children, you must keep the peace here with the people while I go to consider this challenge with Master Zi, the Leader of the Felinia Clowder", Varick said quietly.

Queen Althea nodded to Varick in acknowledgement, before starting to give instructions to Raulf, Sophia and Jai. Just as she started to speak, she was interrupted by Prince Raulf who turned towards his father stating that he would go with them to meet Master Zi. The King agreed, much to Rebel's dismay, as he knew Raulf was not to be trusted. Rebel feared that Raulf's presence at the meeting would not bode well for the discussions.

Rebel quickly led King Varick and Raulf towards the agreed meeting place, along with a small group of the Kings Royal Guard. Rebel made his way down the Mound towards Sheng Forest lighting some orbs on the way down. Rebel had taken the same route he had previously used when he had arrived at the games only a short while ago, as this was the quickest way to the forest. Varick nodded to Rebel in appreciation for the light he had provided, whereas Raulf just frowned and ignored him.

As they approached the forest, Rebel spied Storm moving quietly between the shadows of the trees. Rebel inwardly sighed with relief that Storm was as usual ahead of the game and ready to help if any kind of trouble started. Rebel had come to appreciate Storm and his abilities more and more as time went on. They had become a formidable pair he realised inwardly smiling to himself.

They all quickly made their way through the forest silently following Rebel as he led them deeper into the trees. A short time later they came upon a large clearing where Zi was already seated, others of the Clowder were also present. They were stood in a protective circular formation around the clearing as though they were expecting trouble, Rebel thought to himself.

It was quite dark within the clearing as only the light from the moon, was filtering through between the branches of the trees. Rebel quickly ensured light orbs were spaced evenly around so that all could clearly see each other.

King Varick turned and smiled at him appreciating his thoughtfulness, before making his way to where Zi was sitting.

"Your Majesty", Zi spoke softly, "I am truly sorry about Jonas and the situation he has created. I was only made aware of this challenge a short time before he made it. Unfortunately, it meant that I had no time to persuade him not to make it. Sadly, now the challenge has been made there is no way to stop it. As he has stated, the challenge is correctly made and now we must discuss how to mitigate the damage, not only to the Clowder but also potentially to the family who may lose the Key if the challenge is successful".

The King nodded sighing heavily, "As always you are right Zi, we do indeed have a serious problem on our hands, which now involves everyone in the Kingdom".

Prince Raulf had positioned himself between Rebel and the King, "Father, surely we do not need to honour the challenge. After all it has been made by the Felinia, who are not recognised by the Kingdom. Let us just have him arrested and sent to the dungeons of Druk, people will forget about him and the challenge soon enough", he said with an evil gleam in his eye.

Not surprised at what Prince Raulf had said, Rebel had silently made his way to Storm who now stood at the edge of the clearing. Rebel's mind was full of thoughts and suspicions he did not want to believe about Prince Raulf, unfortunately however a lot of what he had discovered over the last few weeks undercover in the city, were now leaving no doubt in his mind that Prince Raulf had a hand in what was now transpiring.

"Your Majesty, we cannot do that", spoke Zi, "to do that

would be against all that the Heavenly Gate stands for and the Games of the Gods, Shengxiao are for this purpose alone. If you do this, you stand to face the wrath of the Gods and the City of Druk Yul will never recover. As King, you must honour the Games of the Gods and the challenge must be allowed to stand", he said bowing his head as he knelt in front of the King.

"I will do all I can to aid you, Your Majesty, so that peace in the Kingdom is maintained", finished Zi.

King Varick took hold of Zi's shoulders and helped him stand, "You know dear friend that you do not need to bow or kneel to me. We have known each other too long. Let us talk about the Games and what can be done about this challenge".

CHAPTER TWO

The games were based on the Five Earthly Elements, Wood, Fire, Earth, Metal and Water, traditionally the games were open to any family in the Kingdom who wanted to take part and attain a Key.

The Games of the Gods were devised by the Gods to choose those families who could live in the Kingdom and protect the Heavenly Gates. There were twelve keys available which had been held by the current Twelve Chosen Families since the Games began many centuries ago. This was the first time a direct challenge had been made, thus too many unknowns had now been raised.

King Varick was silent as he paced the clearing slowly pondering on the situation. He noticed Rebel talking to a man he did not know, but it was evident the man belonged to the Felinia Clowder. As King Varick approached them, Storm disappeared into the forest as Rebel turned to face the King.

Prince Raulf had also made his way towards Rebel, "Who was that you were talking to Rebel?" he said harshly, "Who was that man? He is clearly from the Felinia Clowder. Father how do we know that Rebel and this man are not involved in this. For all we know Rebel could be the leader of this revolt", Raulf finished with a growl in his voice. Prince Raulf's aura had also started to flare around him, glowing intermittently with a tinge of blue.

Rebel turned to face Raulf, his own aura glowing bright like sunlight, tensions now were running extremely high between them.

"Raulf, BE QUIET", the King responded in a steely voice. "You forget yourself and to whom you are talking about and to", the King gave Raulf a look that brooked no argument and turned to Rebel. "Walk with me" instructed the King.

Rebel gave a backward glance to Raulf, at the same time allowing his aura to fade, as he followed his King to the other side of the clearing. "Rebel, I need you to go back to the Mound and use all your contacts to find out what you can about Jonas and his supporters. This challenge could change everything that the Kingdom stands for if Jonas and the Felinia Clowder do manage to gain a Key. This must not happen, we have to find a way to prevent this from happening", Varick spoke earnestly to Rebel.

Rebel bowed low to his King acknowledging what was required of him before quickly heading in the same direction as Storm into the forest, quickly disappearing out of sight.

The King then turned towards his son, "Raulf go back to your mother and help her", "But father", Ralph started to protest, "GO Ralph", the King spoke sternly. Varick for the second time that evening turned his back to Ralph as he walked towards Zi.

Raulf bristled at the way he was spoken too by Varick. Not only had his father turned his back on him not once but twice in a short space of time, he had done so in front of everyone making him even more angry and resentful.

Raulf contained his anger giving a hateful glance towards his father before making his way out of the forest towards the direction of the Mound.

"Zi my friend let us talk" spoke the King as he sat down on the ground facing him. "We have been solving problems together for too many years Zi, do you think there will ever come a time when there are no problems for us to solve", spoke the King wryly.

"No, your Majesty, I do not, such is the nature of our roles in this world, anyway what would we do if we had no problems to solve", Zi whispered quietly to his friend.

"So, Jonas and his challenge, this is a problem indeed", stated the King. "We both agree that the challenge is valid and therefore stands. The question is how we manage it to our advantage Zi?"

Zi looked thoughtfully at the King, "We know that the challenges within the Games involve the five earthly elements and of the five, Water is the most disliked by the Felinia, Fire is second to this. One way to narrow the chance of Jonas getting to the next stage of the games is to use these two elements first".

"For Jonas to take part in the games he must have a partner, and if I remember correctly, that partner can be chosen by either the Clowder or by the King" ... Zi pondered slowly, "and as yet your Majesty, you have not announced the games and their formation, so we still have time to change the games to our advantage".

"Yes Zi, you are right I can change the games, but I have

a question for you… "Why are you against the Felinia gaining a Key, they are your people Zi?", said the King slightly puzzled, although deep down the King thought he knew the answer, but he wanted to hear it from Zi.

"You are right your Majesty they are my people, and I know them all too well. We as a people are already fractured into many groups, like the Glaring that Jonas is from. We cannot even resolve our own issues so how can we guard the Heavenly Gates. We cannot, I cannot allow the Gates to be exposed to any weakness, and that weakness cannot come from my people, they will not survive if the Gates were to fall due to their failure to protect them. I will do all in my power to stop that happening even if it means that Jonas is thwarted somehow in winning a Key then that's what should happen", Zi spoke passionately as he answered the Kings question.

King Varick patted Zi's shoulder nodding slowly in agreement, "Wise are your words Zi, and well-spoken. Let us focus now on the solution", he said with determination.

"You there", Varick pointed towards one of his guards, "Send this message to the Queen that before the rising of the sun I will come to announce my decision on the games. Until then, let the people celebrate and enjoy the night. Take this and show it to the Queen, so she knows the message is from me", Varick said as he removed a gold signet ring imprinted with the image of a man wearing a crown, imprinted on top of an image of a dragon wearing a crown, from the forefinger of his right hand. He handed it to the Guard, "Be swift", Varick instructed the guard.

"Your Majesty it will be done", replied the guard as he bowed low to his King before turning to walk quickly out of the forest.

Varick turned back to Zi, "We have only a few hours before dawn my friend we must find a way".

Raulf had not gone back to the Mound as instructed but had instead hidden behind a tree to listen to what was being said. Unbeknown to his father the King, Raulf himself was behind the challenge as Rebel had suspected much to Raulf's annoyance.

Raulf had spent the last year trying to find a way to get inside the Heavenly Gates and access all that was held beyond. The only way he could do that was to get a Key, and the only way he could get a Key quickly was through a challenge at the Games.

The announcement of the Games taking place in the traditional way had been made by the King a few months ago. Once this announcement had been made, Raulf saw an opportunity of getting a Key and started putting plans that he had been working on for a while into motion. It was all falling into place, now he was about to achieve his dream.... a Key to the Heavenly Gates and all the riches therein and possibly even the Crown itself.

What nobody knew, was that Raulf was also behind the murders of the High Elders of the Ratticus Family.

Raulf had spent months spreading discontent in the Kingdom and as he did so, sometimes disguised, he had found unexpected allies. Allies that would help him get what he wanted.

In particular, he had been surprised to find allies within the Serpentes Nest. This was going to be extremely useful he thought to himself. Jonas from the Glaring had been most eager, as Jonas, like Raulf wanted power. Only in his case he wanted power over the Felinia Clowder by overthrowing Zi, the Leader of the Clowder.

Apparently, every attempt Jonas had made in the past had failed, and when he was approached by Raulf with the promise of helping him to achieve this, he did not hesitate to offer his support to Raulfs' plans.

With the murder of the High Elders of the Ratticus the opportunity of getting a Key for himself was getting closer. The second part of his plan had now been actioned. Jonas had made the challenge as he had been instructed. There was no way back the plan was now in motion, he had to move forward quickly to ensure its' success. Nothing was going to stop him now, not even his father the King, thought Ralph.

As the messenger from the King walked towards the direction of where Raulf was hiding, Raulf moved further behind the tree, so as not to be seen. As he passed Raulf's hiding place, Raulf followed stealthily behind him for a short distance. Before the messenger could reach the edge of the forest Raulf grabbed him from behind flaring his blue aura encompassing the messenger.

The messenger had no chance to scream as he literally disappeared into thin air with a sizzle leaving the smell of burning flesh lingering in the air.

The Kings' ring he had been clutching in his hand dropped to the forest floor. Raulf quickly picked it up, placing it into his coat pocket, before making his way out of the forest. Feeling absolutely no remorse at what he had done Raulf started to make his way up the Mound towards his mother the Queen and his siblings.

Rebel had been mingling amongst the crowd for a short while, when he sensed something was amiss. As he looked around, he spied Storm looking in his direction, at the same time Storm waived Rebel towards the Dias as he continued to move in the same direction, Rebel turned following Storm. As Rebel approached the Dias, he was alarmed to see Prince Raulf standing next to the Queen. Queen Althea was surrounded by all her children and it looked as though she was preparing to make an announcement.

What was more alarming to Rebel was the blue aura flaming from Prince Raulf. The aura had encompassed his siblings and Queen Althea.

"My People, Hear Me", spoke Queen Althea stiltedly. "Your King, my husband has instructed me to tell you that the games will be postponed until the next full moon in four weeks' time. Here is the Royal Signet as proof of his intent. This night please all enjoy and be merry.

We will take our leave from you now", with that the Queen and her children left the Dias walking the opposite direction to Sheng Forest and away from the King. Rebel noticed that Ralph was leading them quickly away and out of everyone's sight.

Alarmed at what was transpiring, Rebel decided to follow them.

As he made his way through the crowd Rebel noticed the twins Drizzle and Crick to his left, "Drizzle if you can hear me make your way to the King in Sheng Forest and inform him of what transpires here. Tell him I follow the Queen, the

Prince and Princess as I fear for their safety", Rebel pushed this thought towards Drizzle and just as quickly he pushed another towards Crick, "Crick, gather the team and wait for my instructions by the Dias", before Rebel quickly disappeared into the crowd.

As soon as the thought from Rebel had entered his mind, Drizzle had left immediately in the direction of Sheng Forest

Storm must have been close to Crick as he was the first one who Crick had come across of the team as he made his way through the crowd looking for the rest of them.

As they approached the Dias, Crick noticed that the Warrior Maids with the remaining Kings Guard had started to argue between themselves.

When they were only a short distance from them, Mercy and Keon joined them, they could all hear Beda shouting, "Where is Queen Althea, where did she go", panic now evident in her voice.

The Kings Guard were looking as alarmed and as surprised as Beda and her Maids, "We do not know, they were here, then they were gone", one of the Guards spoke quickly in a panicked voice.

Crick and Storm tried to calm the situation by giving a quick explanation as to what was transpiring. They instructed Beda and Conall to be ready and alert in case they were needed. In the meantime, they should ensure that no one was made aware of what was occurring and that the pre-games celebrations should continue as instructed by the King.

It suddenly dawned on Rebel as he followed the Queen, that to everyone except him, the Queen and her children had just suddenly disappeared into thin air. The only reason Rebel could 'see' what had happened was because of his magic, only he could 'see' the blue aura that Ralph had used to encompass them which rendered them invisible to everyone but Rebel.

The music started to fade as Rebel made his way behind the group following them silently to wherever Raulf was taking them. As they walked down the Mound, everyone around them continued with the celebrations unaware of what was transpiring.

Rebel tried to follow close behind, but not too close as he wished to remain unobserved by Prince Raulf. As they passed through a thicket of trees half-way down the Mound, the blue aura that was visible suddenly disappeared to Rebels dismay.

Rebel moved forward quickly to see where they had gone, but to no avail. They had vanished, he had no idea where they had gone or how they had disappeared.

Rebel stood still, frustrated as he looked around the area puzzled. The night had gone much darker as the moon had shifted behind some clouds. The breeze had changed to strong gusts that whistled through the trees eerily. Silence encompassed him as he narrowed his eyes trying to focus on anything that may be moving. Nothing, he could see nothing, they had just disappeared.

He dared not use his magic as he wanted to remain unseen by anyone who may be watching. Rebel made a frustrated grunt as made his way quickly back up the Mound to his friends.

As he walked towards the Dias, Rebel looked around, he could see that all were still oblivious to what was happening as they continued to enjoy the party.

There must have been at least a thousand people on top of the mound enjoying the celebrations. This was making it challenging for Rebel as he made his way through the throngs of people. Finally, breaking through, Rebel made his way to the Dias where he could see his friends standing with the King, his guards, and the Warrior Maids.

"Rebel lad", the King shouted across at him as Rebel did a quick jog across the area marked for the games towards the King. "Did you find them?", the King spoke with a voice that trembled with a mixture of anger and fear.

"No, your Majesty, I followed them to the thicket of trees on the other side of the Mound then they just disappeared", Rebel relayed quickly.

"I don't understand your Majesty, Raulf was using his aura, it encompassed the Queen, Prince Jai and Princess Sofia as he led them through the trees, then they just disappeared. It was as if they had been hypnotised by Raulf, they just followed him without protesting. Something is amiss Sire and we need to find out what it is fast".

The King made his way to the Dias, at the same time motioning for the bell ringers to start ringing the bells. As the bells pealed loudly, the music being played slowly stopped with the people all starting to make their way towards the Dias to where the King now stood.

A hush had fallen across the Mound as the crowd stood quietly looking at their King. Varick motioned for the bell ringers to stop ringing the bells before facing his subjects.

"My people I have some grave news for you this night. Your Queen, and our children Prince Jai and Princess Sofia have been abducted against their will by Prince Raulf", the King spoke in a determined voice with barely contained anger.

A murmuring had begun in the crowd with some shouting cries of outrage, "This means the games will be postponed until the next Thunder moon", announced Varick raising his voice to be heard above the noise of the crowd.

The crowd started to shout loudly, disappointment evident in their cries. Some had even started to make their way towards the Dias, with a few drunk and unruly citizens breaking through the cordoned area for the games.

Rebel's concern grew as he saw the potential for an ugly situation to arise, he motioned for his team to move towards the troublemakers and calm them before it became any worse.

The King had noticed Rebel's action and immediately faced the crowd,

"LISTEN TO ME", said the King loudly and firmly, "We must stay calm and unite to find them quickly, I fear for their lives as I believe Raulf has betrayed his family and has allies among you.

Know this, those who stand against the King of Shengxiao, also stand against the will of the Gods of Shengxiao AND punishment will be severe when you are found out… "AND YOU WILL BE FOUND", the King roared the last sentence which reverberated for miles around.

The DRAGON KING had woken up within King Varick. This was a first, it had never happened before, as the people stared in awe as his aura took on the shape of the mighty Dragon King.

Rebel's own aura was flaring a bright white and to his amazement he could feel the dragon in him taking shape and forming around him, although not as mighty as King Varick, it was still a sight to behold. People stood immediately around Rebel and the King backed away, with a mixture of awe, fear, and pride as they witnessed something never witnessed before by anyone in hundreds of years.

Only legend had foretold that this could happen but never in their lifetimes until now had this event occurred. The crowd became completely silent as they watched in awe their Dragon King.

Beda with Conall warily made their way towards King Varick. "Your Majesty", Conall spoke. "We have failed in our duty to you and our Queen", he started to say when the King interrupted him, "Conall, this is no time for recriminations" he roared gently, "It is, however, time for both the Warrior Maids and the Kings Guard to join forces and send search parties out to find them. I put you in charge Rebel, of organising the search", said Varick turning to face Rebel with a look of sadness and pride on his face as he watched the dragon aura around Rebel glow brightly before it faded to a soft glow around him.

"If ever there was a time, that I needed your special skills Rebel lad, it is now", the King had spoken in dragon tongue,

Rebel understood what he had said replying in the same tongue, "I am yours to command my King".

Rebel turned towards Conall and Beda instructing them to organise search teams. ... "I want all teams to be back here at dawn", Rebel finished a short time later.

The King, with a small contingency of the Royal Guard had decided to make their way back to the Palace. As they passed the Forest of Sheng, Zi came towards them mounted on a white stallion.

As he came alongside the King, Zi informed Varick that Jonas had been taken into custody by the Felinia Clowder until it could be proven he was innocent of any crimes against the Queen and the Kingdom.

The King nodded his acknowledgement of the news, "Join us Zi, I could do with your wisdom during this grave situation", the King said quietly.

"Majesty", Zi acknowledged before dropping a few paces behind the Kings' horse.

CHAPTER THREE

Raulf entered the hidden tunnel which had been revealed to him by Nagid of the Serpentes just a week earlier. The hidden entrance was one of many that the Serpentes Nest used to get in and out of their underground city. It was their domain no-one could find the tunnels unless they were shown by one of the Serpentes.

As they made their way down the tunnel, Nagid joined them from another they had passed on their left. He came alongside Raulf, peering silently at the Royal entourage behind Raulf as they made their way deeper into the Nest.

Raulf still held his family within his blue aura, as they followed closely behind him. He turned to look over his shoulder, and he could see his brother Prince Jai staring at him in anger and disbelief that his brother could do such a terrible deed against his family.

As Raulf looked past Jai, he could just about see the faces of his mother and sister in the dark tunnel. Both had tears trickling down their faces, fear showing clearly in their expressions.

They all knew there was no way back for Raulf, he would most likely face dire consequences when he was caught. They also knew that it was inevitable the wrath of the King would come down on his head when that time came.

Raulf turned back to face the direction they were moving in. He had surprised himself with his actions this night. He felt no regrets at what he had done, he had held little love for his family for a long time, but he would try not to harm them. However, if they got in the way of what he wanted then… his thoughts trailed away as he started to focus on the tunnels which were now becoming very confusing. The unpleasant smell of damp and something else was assailing his nostrils which he quickly covered with his hand.

Raulf led them through a warren of tunnels with the aid of Nagid, until eventually Nagid stopped before turning to face a door on his right. "This one is for your brother Prince Raulf", Nagid lisped as he opened the door wide revealing a small room.

The room held a single bed in one corner, with a chamber pot placed at the foot of the bed. On the other side of the room, a table and chair had been set against the wall. A lamp had been lit casting a greenish glow across the room, along with a single goblet with a jug of water on the table. The room had been sparsely furnished but it was functional.

Nagid grabbed Jai by the arm pushing him into the room. It was not an easy task as Jai struggled against him managing to punch him on the jaw as he did so. Nagid was about to respond in kind when Raulf caught his fist shouting, "NO, do not touch him or any of my family, do you hear me", with that he pushed Nagid away from Jai and walked quickly out of the room, with Nagid following close behind.

Raulf could hear his brother shouting his name through the closed door, as he bolted it shut. Ignoring the shout Raulf led his mother and sister further down the tunnels. They had started to descend downwards as he led them deeper and deeper into the warren of the Serpentes Nest.

The unpleasant smell was getting stronger, almost unbearable the deeper they went. "What is that smell?", Raulf asked distastefully wrinkling his nostrils as he spoke to no one in particular.

Raulf had turned towards Nagid as he asked the question when he noticed Nagid's facial expression.

Nagid was angered at how he had been treated, this showed visibly, as his neck muscles had flared outwards stretching his facial features to resemble his ancestry. His nostrils had flattened as his black eyes peered at Raulf in anger.

Raulf stared at him, "Really you think you can scare me with that display, me a Dragonian", Raulf uttered with contempt, at the same time he flared his blue aura a little brighter. Nagid hissed with pain as the blue flare brushed against his body he jumped quickly out of range.

"Do not EVER forget who you are dealing with Nagid. Let this be a reminder", Raulf stared with contempt at Nagid, whose right side of his body was now showing the early stage of dragon-burn.

Raulf knew it would be very painful. It would also take a few days for the pain of dragon-burn to recede. "Open the door Nagid, NOW", Raulf instructed impatiently.

Nagid made his way slowly towards the door, the pain he was feeling from the dragon-burn was overpowering. He had returned to resemble his human self, albeit pain featuring heavily on his facial expression, sweat starting to bead on his forehead as he tried to control it.

As he moved to open the door, he looked at the Queen and Princess, seeing pity on their faces as well as fear. The Serpentes disliked being pitied, making Nagid glare at them with contempt.

The room was identical to the room Prince Jai had been locked in, except it had two single beds placed on opposite sides of the room. In the middle was another table with a lamp, two goblets and a jug full of water. Chamber pots had been placed at the end of each bed.

"Raulf peered into the room before he turned to his mother and sister. "Welcome to your new home" ... Raulf spoke with not a shred of warmth in his voice as he uttered the words.

This time Raulf entered the room first with his mother and sister following still encompassed by his blue aura. As they entered, Raulf slipped behind them quickly before walking back out of the room, closing, and bolting it shut as he did so.

Raulf turned to face Nagid., "Take me to your High Elders", he said firmly. Nagid stared at him for a moment pain still featuring heavily on his face, the sweat was now dripping freely down the sides of his face. Nagid nodded, brushing a hand across his face wiping away the drips of sweat, before slowly turning to walk in the opposite direction to the one they had come, leading Raulf even deeper into the tunnels.

Rebel had organised three search parties which were composed of a mixture of the Kings Guard, the Warrior Maids, and his friends, ensuring he had included someone with magic in each team.

Storm led one of the teams, as they set off on their search, the others on the team looked at Storm warily. Storm was a Felinia Black, known not for their black colouring but for the fact that they were inherently drawn to and were welcomed by those who wielded powerful magic.

The Felinia Black were the elite of the Felinia Clowder because of their special abilities. They protected the Felinia Clowder from any who would harm them. This was particularly important as the Clowder were not one of the Twelve Chosen. Unbeknown to Rebel, Storm worked closely with Zi to thwart any challenges to Zi's position.

Two years ago, Storm had started to feel within him a burning desire to travel. Storm had lived all his life on the borders of the Kingdom of Shengxiao, in an area called the Clusters with the rest of the Felinia Clowder.

One summer he had started feeling restless and this restlessness had slowly grown out of all proportion. So much so that after he had spoken to Zi regarding this, it was decided that he should follow his gut feeling.

Storm left one week later to make his way into the Kingdom of Shengxiao. Unsure which direction he should follow, he allowed his inner sense to guide his feet. It took many weeks of arduous travel and hardship along the way before he finally found himself in the capital of the Kingdom, Druk Yul.

As he entered the gates of the capital, Storm felt the

pull become stronger. The deeper into the city he went the stronger the pull became.

On the evening of his second day in the city, he found himself standing outside a noisy tavern. Storm stood at the main door of the tavern, when some men from behind jostled Storm out of the way to make their way inside.

As the door opened the smell of smoke, sweat and beer wafted out, Storm wrinkled his nostrils with distaste, the strange pull within Storm had become unbearable with the open door.

Storm slowly made his way into the tavern surveying the scene in front of him. It was a big room with a huge open fire burning on the opposite side of the room to where he stood. There must have been at least a dozen tables scattered around the room, most of which were full of people drinking and enjoying the evening.

To the right of where he stood was the bar, with the innkeeper busy handing trays of tankards full of beer to the various serving maids who were wending their way through the tables handing out the drinks.

There was only one large window in the room that was situated to the left of where Storm stood. As his gaze wandered to a table closest to the window, he realised he had unconsciously started to move towards it.

A group of young men and one woman were sitting at the table. All were chatting away when they suddenly burst into laughter. As he walked towards them, Storm noticed the aura of one young man it was shining brightly literally singing to him.

Storm went to stand behind him placing his hands slowly on Rebels' shoulders. Rebel stood turning his head immediately he felt Storm's hands touch him, voicing a protest at the liberty Storm had taken. His friends had also stood up intending to intervene, but as Rebel started to face Storm he stopped and stared at him for a long time, at the same time he motioned with his hands for his friends to sit down again.

"You're a Felinia Black, how did you find me?", Rebel spoke for the first time with a look of surprise and pleasure on his face.

"You were expecting me?", Storm purred the words with pleasure, knowing now he had found his student.

"Yes, I have dreamt that you would come, these dreams have lasted for many weeks", Rebel spoke with laughter in his voice. "Finally, you are here so maybe I can now get a good night's sleep", he finished with a chuckle.

Rebel pulled another chair to the table and sat down beckoning Storm to do the same. "What is your name?", Rebel said looking at Storm with curiosity, "and how did you find me?", he finished with a questioning look on his face.

"I am Storm and as you rightly point out, I am a Felinia Black. That should tell you how I found you, if you are who I think you are", Storm finished mysteriously.

By now the rest of the group were looking on agog at what was being said. The girl in the group started to ask a question when Rebel gave them a look that they all knew, this would be another of Rebel's secrets they were not privy too.

They sighed and stood up, the girl in the group, whom Storm found out later was Mercy said, “Okay we know that look Rebel. We will see you at the usual place usual time tomorrow”, Mercy finished cryptically.

Once they had left the tavern Rebel turned back to Storm, “Let’s get out of here to talk somewhere private”, Storm stood and followed Rebel out of the tavern. Until now that is all that the others knew of Storm.

The team Storm led, comprised of the Royal Guards, Warrior Maids and High Lord Sylvest who insisted on being part of the search party. His fiancée Princess Sophia was also missing and there was no way he was going to just stand by and not help.

Storm’s team left quickly making their way towards the opposite side of the Mound to Sheng Forest. This was due west to the Capital, and it was also the area where the royals were last seen before they went missing.

The second team was led by Drizzle who was joined by Durai and Fleta. There was a special affinity between Drizzle and Durai, they had been friends for a long time along with Crick, the three of them were a force to be reckoned with within the Ratticus Family. A small number of both the Warrior Maids were also with them.

The third group was headed by Crick, on his team he had Mercy, Beda and Keon, as well as a small contingency of Royal Guards. This was another formidable team.

The last two groups took the South and North side of the Mound, it was agreed by all to meet on the South side of the mound in a couple of hours. A signal had been agreed that if any of the team found anything, they should make their way back to the top of the mound and sound the bells. With the signal agreed all three groups left immediately.

The whole thing only took a short time to organise, once done Rebel quickly made his way to where the royal horses had been tied up, leaping onto Prince Jai's mount. Rebel also grabbed the reigns for Princess Sofia and the Queens's mounts before galloping towards the Kingdom and the King.

As Storm led his team down the West side of the Mound, he instructed them all to move quietly and to spread out in a line. They silently made a slow-paced walk downwards, scouring the ground looking for clues, making their way towards the cluster of trees where Raulf, the Queen and his siblings had all disappeared.

Storm glanced around at the group he was leading, when he noticed that one of the Kings Guard two persons to his left, was looking agitated and a little wary as they approached the tree cluster. Suspicion aroused Storm slowly made his way across to the guard. As he got closer, he noticed by the guard's features that he belonged to the Serpentes Nest.

The closer Storm got to him, the more agitated the guard became. Storm noted that the guards' eyes had started to change, his neck muscles had also started to flatten into the identifying Serpentes transformation.

"What is your name?", Storm hissed quietly to the guard. The guard looked at Storm warily, "I am Jaba of the Serpentes", he lisped.

“Do you realise that you have started to transform yourself? Why is that? What are you not telling us?”, Storm growled.

Jaba hesitated looking even more scared as Storm edged closer to him with an angry look on his face… “I asked you a question, answer me?”, … Storm had spoken loudly this time, the others in the group becoming aware of the altercation started to make their way towards them.

“It is not known by many, on this side of the Mound there is one of the entrances to the Serpentes Nest. It can only be found by one of the Nest”, Jaba said hissing as he finished looking around warily. His tongue had slipped out of his mouth, Storm noticed that the end had forked signalling that a full transformation was about to take place.

“Do you know where the entrance is Jaba?”, Storm asked again, by now the others in the group had formed a semi-circle around Jaba and Storm, watching the altercation with keen interest.

Jaba was virtually in full transformation as he became more anxious, “I do but I cannot tell you it will mean death for me”. The last words were more like hisses than words as Jaba transformed fully before anyone could do anything he had slithered away into the undergrowth and vanished.

Storm tried to pounce after him but was not quick enough, the others in the group were so surprised at what was happening that they too were slow in reacting. As they all started speaking at once Storm shouted, “SILENCE”.

Storm faced the group organising them quickly, “Let us

make a thorough search of this area to see if we can find anything, before we head back. Something is not right, and it involves the Serpentes Nest. Jaba was far too scared, so scared that he transformed, which as we know is very unusual as the Serpentes are very slow in their transformational abilities", Storm finished, signalling to all to spread out, he himself headed towards the direction that Jaba had disappeared.

A short while later after a fruitless search Storm announced to the group, that they should make their way back to the South side of the Mound. Storm led them towards the agreed meeting point. As they made their way around the Mound, they could see that the other two groups had arrived with the leaders of the two groups talking to each other, as the rest of the group were sat watching silently.

Storm approached them, "I think we know who may be involved with the abduction of the Queen and her children", he said growling. "We had a Serpentes guard within our group and as we approached the tree cluster he started to transform. When I questioned him, he said that the secret entrance to the Serpentes Nest was on that side of the Mound, he was too scared to tell us for fear of death. Before I could question him further, he had completely transformed disappearing into the trees before we could stop him. This has to be a sign that the Serpentes Nest is involved with Prince Raulf, as this is where Rebel saw the Prince and his family disappear", Storm spoke quickly.

Storm turned to Drizzle who was stood with Durai and Fleta, "Drizzle go back to the tree cluster if anyone can find the entrance it will be someone from the Ratticus Family, take Durai and Fleta as they are the strongest of the Ratticus", Storm then instructed the others to post guards at strategic points around the Mound.

Making sure that all that could be done had been done, Mercy, Beda and Storm made their way back to the palace to report their suspicions to the King.

CHAPTER FOUR

The Capital Druk Yul was situated on the East side of the Kingdom of Shengxiao. Druk Palace itself was surrounded by gardens which were mostly flat with large fields that were laid with only grass. These were used as training areas for the Dragonian Clan as well as areas to land and take flight.

The outer ring of the gardens was surrounded by trees that seemed to touch the sky and were as wide as any road you would find. The trunks of the trees were red in colour and all year round the leaves remained evergreen. Although, splendid in their own right, the Reds actually hid the magnificent splendour of Druk Palace.

The Palace itself had been built with special bricks using the magical Caysand. When the rays of the sun fell upon the palace it glowed golden like the sun itself. It was famed throughout the Kingdom for its beauty and everlasting magical properties of protection for all things living and otherwise that resided within the walls of the palace.

Past the tree line of the Reds the city sprawled outwards in every direction as far as the eye could see. The city had been divided into twelve sections and each was home to one of the Families who held one of the Twelve Keys of Shengxiao. Looking down from the heavens the Kingdom resembled the shape of the Circle of Time as each section was a different colour. The Palace was at the centre of the

Kingdom with the Reds framing a circle around it.

Shengxiao was a colourful Kingdom with a mixture of buildings having been built over the years in the different sections according to the needs of the residing families. A central courtyard with a miniature version of the palace had been built just facing Druk Palace where the High Elders regularly met and where the Library of Shengxiao was also housed.

This building was called the Peoples Library and was also built using Caysand. The protection of the sand in the bricks ensured that the books remained in perfect condition. Some of the oldest books on its shelves were so precious that if taken out of the library, they would disintegrate as soon as they left the safe confines of the building.

This was well known by all who used the library, so no books were ever allowed out and all who used the library had to read the books within its walls. This was where Princess Sofia spent a lot of her time during the day and the people of the Kingdom often saw her reading and taking notes speaking little so engrossed was, she in her work.

Rebel caught up with the King as they rode past the Peoples Library, announcing that he needed to go inside and turned to Zi to ask him to come too. The last time he had been in the library was when he was talking to Princess Sofia and she was researching something that had caught Rebel's attention. It was this that he needed to re-visit, and he needed Zi's help to do this.

The King nodded his assent to Rebel and continued to make his way to the palace with the rest of the King's Guard.

As Rebel turned towards the library he handed the reigns of the two horses he had brought with him to the nearest guard, with instructions to the guard to make sure the horses of Princess Sofia and Prince Jai were groomed and well-fed as soon as they reached the stables. The guard nodded giving a salute at the same time and took the reigns' before he trotted after the King and his retinue.

As King Varick entered the palace grounds he could see that some of the High Elders of different families had already arrived and were waiting for him.

The King galloped towards the stables and leapt of his horse with the rest of his Guard following suit. Varick quickly made his way towards where the High Elders gathered, "My lords a grave situation has arisen. My Queen and my children Jai and Sofia have been abducted by Prince Raulf. As yet little is known as to the reason behind this, so we must work quickly to find out what plot is afoot here. I fear it has to do with the one available Key to the Heavenly Gates". As he spokes Varick had led them into the Palace and had started to make his way to the Contemplation Hall which was situated at the centre of the palace.

As he walked, Varick had multiple thoughts running through his mind, and he knew that the Contemplation Hall was the place that would help him figure out what needed to be done.

As he thought about the Contemplation Hall his mind wandered to the fact that only a small group of people knew about its true purpose....

The Contemplation Hall mirrored the city of Shengxiao. It was a place of quiet and solitude and large enough to hold nearly a hundred people comfortably. The room was circular in shape and the walls had been divided into twelve separate sections with tall columns from floor to ceiling splitting each section. Each section was covered with white screens, on each screen a single word was written.

The words, Zishi, Choushi, Yinshi, Maoshi, Chenshi, Sis-hi, Wushi, Weishi, Shenshi, Youshi, Xushi, and Haishi. They were the names of the Gods of the Council of Omni.

This was also known as the Circle of Time and each screen represented one of the Chosen Twelve Families. Above each word was an image of the animal representing each word of the Circle of Time.

The floor of the hall was also designed as a circle with twelve sections and each section also had the words written within them. The design on the floor was very intricate and made from the wood of the Reds. Each word had been laid with Caysand and they glistened as the light from the morning sun filtered through the windows giving the room an ethereal glow.

What many didn't know was the meaning of the Circle of Time and what it represented. This knowledge was known only to the Chosen Twelve who held the Keys. The biggest secret was that the Contemplation Hall was also the only way to get to the Heavenly Gates and again only the Key holders were privy to this knowledge.

What was known by all, was that the Circle of Time was all powerful and the words on the screens and on floor represented the will of the Gods. Nobody could stand against the will of the Gods.

The Twelve Chosen Families in the Kingdom were the Ratticus, Oxbow, Panthera, Leporidae, Dragonian, Serpentes, Equidae, Bovidae, Simian, Gallus, Canis and Suidae. It had always been this way, as long as King Varick could remember as he looked at the screens on the walls. To disrupt the Circle of Time would herald the end of the Kingdom of Shengxiao and the challenge for the Ratticus Key was just the beginning.

The King came out of his reverie and turned to the gathered High Elders, ... "My lords we have entered a time of grave danger for our Kingdom and we must make sure that we do not allow anything to happen to the Circle of Time. If the Circle of Time is disrupted it will mean the end of the Heavenly Gates and the Kingdom", the King finished speaking as he looked at the familiar faces gathered around him.

The High Elders started to turn and look at each other, some with concern, others with accusatory looks at other members. One High Elder stood at the back of the gathering unnoticed and stared directly at the King.

King Varick's awareness suddenly went on high alert as he started to feel a prickly sensation all over his body. He scanned his eyes across the room at those gathered when his eyes finally locked with the those of Manasa, High Elder for the Serpentes Nest. They stared at each other for what seemed like an age when suddenly, Manasa started to transform.

The King watched in fascination as those standing around her started to back away some in fear and others with a mixture of disgust and anger as it was taboo to change in front of the King.

When Manasa's transformation was reaching completion, the King gasped, as realisation set in at who he was looking at. Manasa had become Shahmaran, Queen of Serpents. She was the most beautiful woman he had ever seen. As she fully completed her transformation, he could see that below the waist her serpent body had coiled around, so she sat on top majestically and towered above all others in the room.

Shahmaran had long black hair which had been plaited into many braids. White jasmine flowers were weaved into the braids and Varick could smell their perfume from where he stood. Eyes almond shaped were outlined in black and framed by long lashes. A sensuous mouth blood red in colour formed a small pout. Around her neck many gold necklaces nestled on her bosom. Dressed in a flowing green top which glistened and shimmered in the sunlight. Shahmaran was breathtakingly beautiful.

Her arms held golden bangles from her wrists to her elbows, in the middle of her forehead was a golden snake which started from the parting in her hair to the middle of her eyebrows. Shahmaran's eyebrows curved all the way across her eyes and ended with two diamonds at the end of each eyebrow. She looked every bit the regal Queen she was.

The rest of her snake body was olive in colour with yellow stripes down the full length of the underside of her tail. The stripes running down the belly of the tail identified Shahmaran as the Queen of the Serpentes.

"Your Majesty, I must apologise for transforming here in

the Contemplation Hall, but I had no choice but to reveal myself due to the gravity of the situation. May I ask your Majesty's leave to request all the other High Elders to leave the room". Shahmaran spoke with a commanding but gentle voice that had a slight endearing lisp.

Others in the room started to protest at the liberty, and were still taken aback by what had transpired, but King Varick spoke firmly whilst still mesmerised by Shahmaran. "Leave us, all of you". Varick said with authority.

Unintentionally King Varick's dragon aura had appeared and was a towering presence in the room. The room had become even brighter as the sun had now risen high in the sky, sunlight filtering through to reach every corner of the room.

"This is a first Shahmaran". Spoke the King deferentially after all had left the room, "I had been told that you may be residing on earth but no confirmation of this had ever been made".

"You are right Varick I have kept myself hidden for a reason, and the reason is now apparent. Many moons ago I had been informed that the Serpentes had a challenger within the Nest. This has never happened before in the history of the Serpentes and I wanted to know why and who had made this challenge". Shahmaran had slowly and gracefully made her way across to Varick and had curled up next to where he was now sat. She spoke slowly and thoughtfully as she leaned towards him…

"At first I thought the challenge was against me and I needed to find out who the opponent was. However, I have found that the challenge is actually against you Varick.

The only way that the challenge can be made against you is through the games and by getting hold of one of the Keys. Sadly, I bring bad tidings to you that the challenger is as I think you are now beginning to realise, your own son Prince Raulf.

My involvement has been necessary as he has used some of my followers in the Serpentes Nest to be his allies. I must protect the Serpentes Nest at all cost, so I will help you Varick to stop Prince Raulf from getting a Key", she finished with a hissss and a slight bow to King Varick.

Rebel and Zi entered the Peoples Library and looked around in awe as all did when they entered. The Library was magnificent and was much larger than the outside portrayed. That was the magic of the Caysand it appeared small outside but inside it was huge and had been constructed with four defining pillars.

They were called the Pillars of Destiny and within each pillar held the books of the past, the present and those that foretold the future of three of the twelve families. Each of the group of three were called a Trine and there were four Trines in total.

The first trine belonged to the Ratticus, Dragonian and Simian families.

The second trine housed the family history of the Oxbow, Serpentes and Gallus. The third trine Panthera, Equidae and Canis and finally the fourth Leporidae, Bovidae and Suidae.

The librarians were also special in their abilities as they were handpicked to represent every family within the Kingdom. Their primary duty was to look after their own family Histories.

Rebel led Zi towards the pillar marked First Trine, as they approached the entrance, the huge door which protected it swung open. Both walked in slowly, awed at the sight before them as they gazed at the sheer number of books on shelves which housed them.

There were three walls as the pillars were triangular in shape and each wall was allocated to a family. Rebel made his way to the wall that held the family history of the Dragonians, with Zi following closely behind him.

"What are we looking for Rebel?" spoke Zi.

"When last I was here Princess Sofia was researching the history of the dragon auras and how they are created. Also, we were trying to find out why each dragons' aura is different. At the Kings' request Princess Sofia was looking into Prince Raulf's aura in particular, as it is the only one that we are aware of that has a blue tinge to its edges". Rebel explained.

"What concerns me," Rebel continued... "is that Raulf used his aura tonight to take control of the Royal Family, so it seems it is even more imperative that we find out about his aura and its capabilities", ...Rebel finished. As he did so the librarian for the section arrived.

"Rebel good to see you again, how can I assist you today? If you are looking for Princess Sofia she has not arrived yet, I have just come from where she usually sits", Librarian Xin finished with a smile.

"I bring bad tidings sir, Princess Sofia, the Queen and Prince Jai have been abducted by Prince Raulf. I am here to look at the last few books that the Princess was using for her research. Please could you get them for us as a matter of urgency", Rebel spoke quickly and made his way towards where Sofia normally sat beckoning Zi to come with him. Shocked at hearing the news, Librarian Xin quickly disappeared to do as he was asked.

A short while later Librarian Xin appeared with a pile of books in his arms and placed them on the table in front of Rebel and Zi. "These are all the ones Her Highness was looking at. If you care to tell me what you are looking for perhaps, I can help you find the information more quickly", he finished gravely.

"Pull up a seat Xin and look for the book with a cover of the image of a dragon imprinted on top and the image of a man printed on top of the dragon. That is the Book of Auras and I think we may find the answers we are looking for in there. Sophia and I were very close to finding the answer and I'm hoping that Master Zi can help us to discover the reason behind the blue tinged aura", finished Rebel as he went through the books Xin had brought.

Very quickly Xin found the book Rebel was speaking of and noticed that a piece of paper was sticking out of the middle of the book. Xin opened the page marked with the paper and saw that the paper had notes written on it in the Princess's hand. He quickly handed the paper to Zi.

Zi started to read what was on the paper and every now and again would start muttering something to himself... "Zi what does it say", Rebel said impatiently after ten minutes of watching Zi muttering to himself.

"It is not good news Rebel, according to Sophia's notes the blue tinge is from Earth's Internal flame and only shows itself rarely in the aura of a dragon. No one really knows why a dragon is chosen with this aura, but that the one chosen has powers beyond the normal auras of dragons and can be used for good or evil. In your brother case it seems he has chosen to take the path of evil", Zi finished trailing his words and eventually going silent but kept looking at the paper.

"Sofia has written something else, but I cannot decipher it", Zi spoke again looking up at Rebel.

"Let me see", Rebel said as Zi passed the paper over to him. Xin was sitting quietly listening to all this when he suddenly stood up. "Oh, my goodness I nearly forgot, there is one other book that Her Highness was looking at, but it is currently on loan to the Second Trine at the request of the Serpentes Librarian Zora. She asked to borrow it only yesterday and that particular book is called, "The Colors of Flamecore", he finished hurriedly.

Rebel looked up at Xin a frown marring his features.

"Librarian Xin, please make your way quickly to the Second Trine and request the return of the book by order of the King", Rebel said firmly.

Looking at Zi. "I think Master Zi, the answer to the last notes written by Sophia will be in the missing book. Let us hope that Xin will bring it back here quickly", Rebel finished as he ushered Xin away and giving Xin a look that said don't fail.

CHAPTER FIVE

Raulf had been walking for quite a while in the dark tunnels and was starting to get irritated. Raulf had noticed that his aura had been flaring for a while and the blue tinge was getting brighter the deeper into the tunnels he went. Not only that, he was also feeling something changing inside him, and he couldn't quite put his finger on it.

What he did know, was that he could suddenly switch his aura on and off like his brother Jai with just a thought. This was definitely something new, as it normally took him a good five minutes to build up his power from within to transform. He made mental notes of the changes that were occurring within him as he followed behind Nagid.

After nearly an hour in the tunnels Nagid stopped in front of two enormous doors on which the image of Shahmaran the Queen of Serpents, had been carved. The carving was magnificent with gold etched on the image where the Queen wore her jewels. Two large diamonds glistened at the end of each beautifully curved eyebrow and carved in gold on her forehead the image of a serpent. The everlasting fragrance of jasmine emanated from the doors a constant reminder of Shahmaran's favourite flower.

Two Black Cobra Serpentes Guards were stood outside the doors in their snake form and Raulf could feel their black eyes peering at him in the dark.

"Prince Raulf of the Dragonian Clan is here to see the High Elders, open the doors", hissed Nagid loudly.

The Black Cobra guards did not hesitate as it was royalty, pushing the doors inwards until they were fully open, revealing a huge cavern beyond. The cavern walls were illuminated by a fluorescent green light making the cavern look eerily dark. At the far end was a huge statue that nearly reached the ceiling which was easily one hundred feet in height.

The statue was of Shahmaran, surrounding the base of the statue were small miniature bushes of jasmine, the tiny white flowers looking green in the fluorescent light of the cavern. Surrounding the statue were many of the Serpentes Nest all in snake form and all curled up looking trancelike at the statue of Shahmaran.

"Where are the High Elders Nagid I cannot see them here?". Raulf said as his gaze wandered at all those gathered in the cave.

"I do not know Prince; something must have happened as I have never seen so many Serpentes gathered like this in their snake form before". Nagid hissed quietly.

As they moved further into the cave one slithered towards them and slowly shifted back to its human form.

"My Prince I am Jaba of the Royal Guard, and I have just escaped the search party that was looking for the Queen, Prince Jai and Princess Sofia. They were close to the entrance and unfortunately the Felinia Black called Storm has discovered that the Serpentes are involved in your plan", hissed Jaba bowing his head as he continued speaking.

"I am sorry my Prince I could not stop myself from transforming when he approached me as I knew with his powers, he would be able to force me to reveal the entrance to the Nest".

Jaba was still speaking when Raulf, in anger expanded his blue aura, Jaba gave a blood-curdling scream as he disappeared in a puff of smoke. The smell of burning flesh permeated around the cave overpowering the perfume of the Jasmine.

Nagid stood rigid with shock and spoke with a hint of fear in his voice. "Why Prince Raulf did you do that? He was trying to help us".

Raulf gave Nagid a look so disdainful that Nagid stepped back from Raulf and bowed his head in deference… "I am sorry my honourable Prince for daring to question you. It will not happen again", Nagid finished quietly and kept his eyes lowered.

Whilst all this was occurring Raulf had failed to notice that the Serpentes in the cave had all uncoiled and were now back in human form and bowing to the statue of Shahmaran. A hush had fallen in the cave, the light in the cave had become even brighter so much so that you could now see clearly all who had gathered. All of them were looking up at the statue. Raulf followed their gaze and what he saw made him drop to his knees along with Nagid.

The statue of Shahmaran had opened her eyes and was

looking directly at Prince Raulf. That's when Raulf realised he had made his first mistake. He had just killed a Serpentes in the temple of the Serpentes in front of many from the Nest. Not only that, he had done it in front of the altar of Shahmaran. It was an unforgivable mistake one that he was now beginning to regret.

Nagid was also looking at Shahmaran, and as he did, he noticed that she was staring at Raulf.

Nagid slowly started to slither backwards, to put distance between himself and Raulf, at the same time he had also noticed that all in the room had turned to follow Shahmaran's gaze and were staring at Raulf with looks of disbelief and anger.

As Raulf was about to speak Shahmaran silenced him, "Do not speak Prince Raulf, you have committed a grave sin in killing one of the Serpentes, and penance MUST be paid", she hissed and as she did her tongue forked out of her mouth and without warning she spat poison directly at Raulf.

Before Raulf could move white mucous hit him squarely on the chest and slowly started to spread. As it did Prince Raulf could feel his arms and legs slowly seize up. Raulf quickly flared his aura and the blue flame sizzled bright as it started to burn away the poison on his body. Raulf noticed that as it did so, his aura had become completely blue dazzling all in the room.

"Do not threaten me Shahmaran. You do not know with whom you are dealing with", roared Raulf whose blue aura had started to shape into his dragon. Raulf's dragon was a dazzling blue and as big as the statue of Shahmaran.

Raulf had surprised himself as he had never been able to awaken the dragon within. He hid his surprise and turned to face Shahmaran. "You will listen to me and you will help me", he roared...

"I want the Key and you will help me get it, otherwise all in the Nest will die", he flamed his aura to touch those nearest to him, and they burst into flames screaming before disappearing into thin air.

The smell of burning was heavy in the air and all the others had started to move backwards only stopping when they reached the walls of the cave where they cowered fearing Raulf's dragon aura.

"Your answer Shahmaran?" Raulf growled in his throat at the same time a blue flame burst from his dragon mouth to the surprise of both Shahmaran and Raulf.

"You will get my answer on the next day's eve. DO NOT FORGET TO WHOM YOU SPEAK". Shahmaran hissed loudly, with that she closed her eyes. The statue of Shahmaran now held a look of frozen anger on her face.

Shahmaran opened her eyes again, facing her now was King Varick. King Varick had been staring at Shahmaran with consternation, as only a short time ago in the middle of talking she had closed her eyes and had gone into a trance.

Coming back just as suddenly she spoke, "I am sorry your Majesty, Prince Raulf has committed a grave sin against the Serpentes, and he has challenged me to help him. If I do not, he will destroy the Serpentes Nest", Shahmaran hissed.

Varick looked aghast at Shahmaran, "What has he done?", Varick growled.

"He has killed in the temple of Shahmaran many of the Serpentes. But this is not all, his aura is so strong that it has formed into a blue dragon of immense size, and he is now able to breathe blue fire. It seems that being underground has somehow increased his power with such levels that we cannot fathom yet."

Silence filled the air after that statement then Shahmaran spoke again with passion, "We must find a way to stop Prince Raulf and quickly before he not only destroys the Nest but also your family and the Kingdom if he gets hold of a Key", she hissed her tongue darting out of her mouth as she spoke. At the same time, she took hold of Varick's hand bowing her head low, "we face difficult times ahead Varick, you most of all will be challenged as the culprit is your son"

Librarian Xin was making his way towards the entrance of the second Trine when he saw the doors of the Trine start to close. Surprised as there was still daylight outside, and the doors were normally closed at dusk, Xin quickened his steps into a run. They were nearly closed shut as he reached them, Xin pushed hard against them to prevent them from closing fully.

"Librarian Zora" he shouted, "why are you closing the doors so early, is there something wrong?", Xin spoke hurriedly. Silence greeted his statement.

"You must return the book you borrowed yesterday immediately, by order of the King", Xin shouted as he continued to push against the doors.

"Zora, Zora what is wrong, where is the book?", he shouted, as he pushed, he lost his footing and slipped face down flat onto the floor. The door banged shut, and he could hear the bolts being pushed into place on the other side.

Quickly Xin stood up and started to bang on the door loudly, "Zora OPEN UP THE DOORS", he shouted even louder. By now, others in the library had started to come out of the various columns to find out what all the fuss was about.

Rebel on hearing the commotion came running out with Zi close behind him. "Librarian Xin, what is wrong? Where is the book?", Rebel questioned as he took in what was happening.

Rebel stared at the locked doors and then looked at Zi. "I think the answers we are looking for are definitely in that book". At the same time Xin spoke anxiously to both of them, "I don't understand she heard me and saw me coming, and she still continued to shut the doors, Zora wouldn't let me in".

"The Colors of Flamecore! I thought that book to be lost", Zi spoke quietly.

"Yes, indeed I can see why the Serpentes do not want us to get hold of this book, it contains the knowledge to the Auras of the Dragons and in the wrong hands it is an extremely dangerous book. Unfortunately Rebel it is now in the wrong hands", Zi finished looking at Rebel gravely.

"We must go now to the Palace and notify King Varick of what has transpired Rebel, and we must do so quickly as I fear if Raulf gets hold of this book, it will be very easy for him to get one of the Keys to the Heavenly Gates" Zi had started to move towards the door that would take him back outside the Peoples Library.

As they were walking out, Mercy, Beda and Storm were walking in.

"How did you know I was here Storm? Never mind don't answer that, it's a stupid question of course you know where I am. Anyhow, I have another task for you Storm. Librarian Zora of the Second Trine has stolen a book from the First Trine. It is called 'The Colors of Flamecore'. I need to you to find Zora and the book and bring them both to me at the Palace. Beda, I want you to go with Storm, Mercy you come with me". Rebel continued to walk outside and was already mounting his horse as he was finishing speaking.

Before Rebel left, Storm and Beda gave him a brief summary of what had transpired at the Mound with the search parties. This now left no doubt in Rebel's mind that Raulf and the Serpentes were behind the abduction of the royal family and the plot to get a Key.

After they had finished their brief report, Storm and Beda made their way back into the library and were met by Librarian Xin who started to fill them in on what had transpired so far.

Rebel, Mercy and Zi now galloped towards the palace to meet with the King. As they entered the palace one of the Kings Guard told them that King Varick was in a meeting in the Contemplation Hall.

As they approached the Contemplation Hall, they noticed

that Elders of the other Families were huddled in groups just by the entrance to the Hall. Rebel also noticed that the doors were closed shut. Rebel could hear raised angry voices coming from some of the Elders.

Rebel made his way towards the doors with Zi and Mercy…

““You cannot enter the King has asked us all to wait outside he is talking to Shahmaran, Queen of Serpents”, one of the Elders called out to them.

Zi stopped suddenly in his tracks upon hearing this and looked towards the doors of the Contemplation Hall, “I cannot enter Rebel, you go and tell the King all you know”, spoke Zi quietly.

“Why Zi what is wrong?”, Rebel looked at Zi in surprise.

“Know that Shahmaran and I have a difference we need to resolve, one that must be resolved in private. In me trust Rebel”, ... with that Zi turned and started to walk back the way they had come. “I will wait for you Rebel at the Stables come to me when you have finished, do not FORGET to come to me”, Zi finished cryptically as he went around the corner and out of sight.

Mercy looked at Rebel “What was all that about Rebel?” “I don’t know Mercy, but go with Zi and wait for me”, with that Rebel turned and walked towards the doors of the Contemplation Hall.

As Rebel opened the doors, he heard a female voice, as he entered, he could see the King sat down with a Serpentes female next to him, and she was holding his hand.

"Rebel lad close the door behind you and come to us", Varick spoke quietly as he saw who had entered the room.

As Rebel closed the doors, he noticed the faces of those gathered outside were trying to peer into the Hall to see what was happening. Rebel closed the doors with a loud thud and slid the bar across the door to stop anyone from entering. He then made his way to where the King was sitting and bowed low but kept his eyes on whom he believed was Manasa High Elder of the Serpentes.

"Majesty, I must report to you in private", ... Rebel spoke quietly but firmly.

"Rebel let me introduce you to Shahmaran, Queen of the Serpentes", Varick spoke with reverence looking at Shahmaran.

"But your Majesty this is Manasa Elder of the Serpentes not Shahmaran!" As Rebel finished speaking the features of Manasa changed. Now sitting in front of him was Shahmaran.

Rebel gasped in awe as he had heard of the history of Shahmaran, but never thought he would ever meet her she was more beautiful than history had foretold. He was mesmerised with her beauty.

"Master Rebel, to all who look upon me I am Manasa, only those whom I wish, can see my true self. Please report to King Varick and me what you have learnt, and we can then let you know what has transpired since last you were with the King", Shahmaran lisped quietly.

Rebel bowed low to Shahmaran and his King in acknowledgement, before he relayed what had happened during the search on the Mound. Rebel finished by saying that they suspected Raulf was mixed with the Serpentes in his hopes to gain a Key, looking at King Varick with sadness as he spoke.

He then relayed that Zi had been helping him figure out the research Princess Sofia had been doing and that the book "The Colors of Flamecore", probably held the answers they were looking for, but it had gone missing or had been stolen.

Rebel finished by saying that Storm and Beda were currently looking for Librarian Zora and the book. Once they had found it, they would report back here at the palace.

As he was speaking both Varick and Rebel noticed that Shahmaran had started to move towards the window where she stood still, gazing out with a frown marring her features.

"Zi is here?", she said turning around to look at Rebel.

"Yes, your Majesty, he waits for me at the stables", Rebel looked at Shahmaran and then the King. Shahmaran said nothing else and went back to where Rebel was standing looking directly into his eyes, she said, "You are correct in your assumptions young Rebel, the Serpentes are indeed involved. As yet I do not know who Raulf has as allies within the Nest, but know that he has made many enemies this night by killing many of the Serpentes in the Temple of Shahmaran, and he did so in front of me".

Shahmaran hissed loudly, "Revenge will be ours Varick, you know that you must forfeit your son's life for the sins he has committed".

Varick looked at Rebel with sorrow in his eyes, "Shahmaran is right Rebel lad, but first we must find my Queen, Jai and Sofia. We must have them safe before we can deal with Raulf". Looking at Shahmaran he continued, "Only you can help us find the entrance to the Serpentes Nest, Shahmaran. Will you help us do this so we can save my family? I promise once my family is back here safe with me, we will deal with Raulf".

Shahmaran looked at King Varick, then at Rebel and nodded slowly, "Yes, I will help you Varick, but only a small group must enter the Nest, and then they must vow not to reveal the entrance to anyone ever", she finished with a hiss facing Varick.

Varick looked at Rebel and then at Shahmaran, "Agreed. Rebel lad you must be the one to lead the group into the Nest, know this is a grave responsibility I place on your shoulders. Will you do this?", Varick looked at Rebel with sadness emanating from his eyes.

"Majesty, yours to command", Rebel faced his King, ... "I will do all I can to bring Queen Althea, Prince Jai and Princess Sofia back to you safely". Rebel turned to look at Shahmaran, "I am saddened to hear what has happened in the Nest and defer to your advice on how many should be in the group that enter the Nest, Queen Shahmaran. I will do all I can, to complete this mission safely and quickly", Rebel finished with a low bow and fire in his eyes.

"A good choice Varick, the boy has spirit. No more than four Rebel", she continued, "and in that group you must include Zi, he will be invaluable to you", she finished cryptically.

"Rebel who else will you take with you, there is no time to waste as time is of the essence", Varick finished. "As well as Zi, I will take Mercy and Drizzle from the Ratticus. Drizzle should be able to communicate with his twin brother Crick via mind meld for obvious reasons as we go into underground tunnels."

Rebel finished speaking and looked at Shahmaran, "Prepare yourselves and meet me on the Mound by the Dias in two hours. Queen Shahmaran and I will meet you there, and Rebel lad". Varick put his arm around Rebel's shoulders, "Be careful, do not trust Raulf if you come across him. He has betrayed his family and will not hesitate to betray you any way he can".

CHAPTER SIX

Storm and Beda were now being led by Librarian Xin to the First Trine, as they approached, they could see that a small crowd had gathered outside the locked doors of the Trine. The crowd parted to let them through, there on the floor in a crumpled heap lay Librarian Zora, blood seeping from a wound on her head.

"What happened?" Storm growled, when someone in the crown shouted, "She fell sir, from above, just a few minutes ago".

Storm and Beda looked up and couldn't see where she could have fallen from.

"Beda there is no window, so she couldn't have been pushed nor could she jump. Something else is at work here and I can feel the tingle of used magic in the air. Something very wrong is going on here", whispered Storm. Beda had been scanning the crowd as she listened to Storm, suddenly she started to run towards a cloaked figure which was nearing the exit to the library. "You there, STOP", she shouted.

Storm followed running after her quickly and was only a step behind when suddenly the running figure fell to the floor. They both came to a standstill as they reached the figure, Storm bent down to pull off the cloak which covered the stranger. To their utter amazement the figure had just disappeared into thin air leaving only the cloak behind.

"What just happened Storm?", Beda asked breathlessly looking at Storm and the cloak he was now holding. Storm remained silent staring at the cloak, his face started to harden with anger and a hint of fear, his body was now tingling uncontrollably.

"A lot of magic has been used here Beda, I can still feel the after effects of it," Storm replied, at the same time he removed a coin out of his pocket and threw it towards the door. Beda watched in amazement as the coin just as suddenly disappeared

Looking at Beda he said, "Somebody has opened up a Chaos Portal and it takes powerful magic to do that". Storm handed the cloak to Beda, "Keep hold of this Beda, do not let it leave your sight. It is a Caysand Cloak, the only one in existence that we know of belongs to King Varick. We must make haste to the Palace to speak with the King".

"What about the book?" Beda started to say. "I suspect the book has also disappeared along with the mystery intruder, let us go quickly Beda this is more serious that at first we thought". Storm was now making his way out and walking towards his horse. Beda ran after him, tucking the cloak under her arm as she went.

Raulf was a little disorientated and breathless after travelling through the portal so quickly. Tucked under his tunic close to his chest was the Color of Flamecore wrapped in Caysand fabric. The fabric would hopefully protect the book from disintegrating as it had been removed from the protection of the Peoples Library. To his annoyance the cloak he had been wearing had not come through the portal with him, it had fallen off him as he had entered, and he was not sure why this was the case.

The longer Raulf had remained in the Nest the more powerful he had become. To his utter amazement the knowledge of his ancestors had also started to flood into his mind. It was this knowledge that had made Raulf aware about the book and its importance to helping him succeed with his plans.

Before he could move, a coin tinkled noisily onto the floor next him. Raulf looked at it puzzled, then it dawned on him that Storm had figured out that a portal had been opened. Raulf became annoyed at himself for being reckless, he was hoping to keep that secret a little longer to help him get what he wanted. No matter, thought Raulf, there was nothing Storm could do anyway to thwart his plans.

The knowledge of creating a portal had also come from his ancestors. Raulf had been surprised to learn how easy it had been to create one. Not only that, he could also use the same portal a number of times by just visualising where he wanted to go.

A whole chapter about the Chaos Portals had been written in the Book of Elders, but the knowledge of how to create one had been lost. Now Raulf knew how to do it, he would use it to his advantage. Raulf was aware of the danger of the Chaos Portals. His arrogance, however, made him think he could control them as he was getting stronger by the day.

Raulf turned and made his way out of the temple of Shahmaran, at the same time he instructed Nagid to follow him. Nagid who was sat close by was just staring at him mouth wide open in amazement at how Raulf had just disappeared and then reappeared a short time later.

"Nagid, I need to see my sister Sophia, take me to her", Raulf instructed and strode out into the tunnels. Nagid followed quickly, worry furrowing his brow at what he had witnessed.

Raulf was becoming very dangerous and Nagid was becoming more and more scared at what he had got himself involved in. Keeping his head lowered, Nagid overtook Raulf walking quickly ahead he led him towards the room where Sophia and the Queen were being kept.

A short time later they reached the room and as Raulf entered the room he noticed an unusual odour but couldn't quite place what it was. His mother and sister were sitting holding hands on one of the beds. They looked up at him as he walked in. "Sophia, I need to speak with you regarding the Chaos Portals", Raulf stood towering over them. As he spoke, he noticed Sophia's startled expression when he had mentioned the Chaos Portals. "Ahh, so you know of what I speak, you will help me understand them further Sophia as you also have the knowledge of our ancestors".

"How do you know about the Portals", Sophia whispered with dread in her voice. "That knowledge has been lost, and it was forgotten for a reason, you must not use the Portals Raulf they are dangerous".

"Why are they dangerous, I have already used them, nothing has happened that was dangerous", Raulf said in a superior voice.

"Are you sure nothing happened Raulf?", Sophia answered cryptically.

"What do you mean Sophia?", Raulf spoke impatiently.

"I will tell you only this Raulf, as you are my brother, every time you use a portal, the portal will take something from you", as she finished speaking, she turned away from Raulf and looked at her mother worry marring her features.

Queen Althea looked at Sophia and then to Raulf she said, "Raulf, I do not know why you do this, there is still time to stop this nonsense, nothing has happened yet. Let us go free and I will speak to your father. What of your brother is he safe?", "Mother, you never did understand me" Raulf looked down at his mother and then to Nagid he said, "Bring Sophia with us", as he turned and walked out of the door.

Nagid grabbed hold of Sophia's arm and hauled her up struggling as she tried to wriggle free. "Stop wriggling Princess, I have no choice, your brother is a dangerous man we must do as instructed", he hissed as he dragged Sophia out of the room and slammed the door shut behind him.

Queen Althea had stood up to try and stop him but stopped as she felt her arms and legs stiffen, she fell back onto the bed. As she fell, she looked towards the door and saw Raulf looking at her in concentration, and she saw a blue light in his eyes flare suddenly just as the door slammed shut.

Sophia stared at Raulf as she also caught a glimpse of his eyes and turned away quickly so that Raulf could not see the shock on her face. She started to recall the notes she had made from the book, Colors of Flamecore and realised that

Raulf had started to present some of the signs she had read about.

The more she thought about it the more alarmed Sophia became, not only was Raulf in grave danger, it seems so was the Kingdom of Shengxiao if he wasn't stopped. Raulf did not know what a dangerous game he was playing, she only hoped that someone would find them quickly before it was too late.

Storm and Beda entered the palace and quickly made their way towards the Contemplation Hall. "Storm how do you know where to find Rebel?", Beda asked questioningly as they walked down a long corridor. "I just do", replied Storm and with that he carried on walking. As they turned a corner, they saw a small crowd gathered outside the Contemplation Hall.

As they approached the crowd, the doors to the Hall opened with Rebel, the King and Elder Manasa walking out. Everybody turned as the doors opened, going silent in anticipation of finding out what was happening.

"I need you all to wait in the Contemplation Hall until I return. Food and drink will be prepared for you. When I return, I will answer all your questions! Know that all is in hand", Varick finished in a voice that brooked no argument.

Those who were about to protest stopped in their tracks as they saw Manasa staring at them challengingly. Recalling that she was actually Shahmaran, they meekly did as they were instructed, all going silent as they made their way into the Contemplation Hall.

Storm stared at Manasa, who in turn was also looking at

Storm, "Storm, it has been a long time since we met last. It is a pity we have to meet in such circumstances. It is good to see you again my friend", she hissed quietly.

Rebel looked from one to the other and said surprised, ... "You know each other?".

Storm looked at Rebel, "Yes we do, but right now I have some urgent news for you Rebel, and the King", Storm said bowing low to King Varick as he spoke.

"Walk with us Storm and relay the information. Rebel must make his way to Boundary Hill quickly", Varick spoke as he led the way down the corridor.

Storm quickly relayed what had happened at the Peoples Library, as he did so he instructed Beda to hand the Caysand cloak back to King Varick. King Varick looked at it in amazement, "How did you come by this? It was locked away in my quarters".

"The intruder left it behind as he disappeared into the portal, and Storm threw a coin at the portal and it also disappeared", Beda spoke with awe in her voice.

Manasa slowed down and then stopped. King Varick looked at her questioningly and said, "Manasa, what is wrong?"

Manasa looked at Storm and spoke, "A Portal has been opened, you know what this means don't you Storm?", Storm nodded.

Manasa continued, "Then you also know that we now

have to get involved in our true forms. Zi is at the stables we need to go to him, especially if someone has resurrected the Chaos Portals".

"King Varick, Rebel follow me, we must speak to Zi, we cannot let Rebel go into the Nest knowing what we now know", Manasa finished indicating to Rebel to lead them to the stables.

"Why what has happened, what is a Chaos Portal?", spoke Varick.

"All will be revealed your Majesty, trust me in this, not only is your family in grave danger but all the Kingdom has been put into unimaginable danger, one that we could never have foreseen". Manasa had become Shahmaran as shespoke, a hint of fear could be detected in her voice.

Beda looked on in amazement at Shahmaran, realising who she was Beda looked at Storm who gave her a look with a slight shake of his head, that said don't ask just keep walking.

Rebel had always loved the smell of the stables especially when fresh hay had just been laid, and he breathed in deeply as they entered the stables. It brought back memories of his childhood and his father with whom he had spent a lot of time. It was his father who had taught him how to ride and look after the horses, and he missed that, he missed his father and mother and the simple times of his younger days.

Zi was sat on the hay in the centre of the stables, with his eyes closed and head bowed, Mercy was sat near one of the horses stroking its head and looking towards Zi. Rebel made his way to Mercy, "How long has he been like this Mercy?". "Only a short while, we were talking when suddenly he stopped, closed his eyes and lowered his head".

Shahmaran and Storm made their way to Zi and sat down next to him. As they did so Zi opened his eyes and raised his head and looked straight at Shahmaran then he turned his gaze to Storm speaking to them both, "It is good to see you old friends. We have work to do and little time to do it", Zi finished and then looked at Rebel and the King.

"Your Majesty and young Rebel please sit with us. Beda and Mercy guard the doors of the stable do not let anyone in, and I mean ANYONE", Zi spoke quietly but firmly.

Mercy and Beda made their way out of the stables and shut the doors behind them. Both stood guard looking at each other questioningly but kept silent and watchful as Zi had bid them.

"King Varick, Rebel let me start by telling you who we are", said Zi, "I think you have both realised that Manasa is Shahmaran, God Queen of the Serpentes". Varick and Rebel both nodded in unison.

"Storm is a Felinia Black as you know, but what you don't know is that Storm is King of the Felinia Black and as such he is also a valued advisor to the Gods," Zi continued. Zi then nodded to Storm signalling for him to continue.

torm bowed his head in deference to Zi, turning to King Varick and Rebel, "You are in the presence of the God of Age also known as Tai Sui and known to all in the Kingdom as Zi", as Storm spoke he bowed his head to Zi. Both Varick and Rebel were shocked, amazed and daunted at the same time, with the thought of who they were sat in the presence off. They remained silent absorbing what they had just learnt, different thoughts running through each of their minds about what they were being told.

Zi continued looking at Rebel, "It was me who sent Storm to you Rebel. You are an incredibly special person; I knew this when you were born, and it was with my instructions that I asked King Varick to look for you and bring you back to the Kingdom. What you do not know Rebel, is that King Varick is your uncle, your father is his brother". Rebel taken aback and shocked at the revelation, turned towards Varick for confirmation. Rebel could see in Varick's eyes that what Zi had said was the truth. Zi continued, "I know you will have many questions young Rebel, but now is not the time to ask or seek answers to those questions.

Know that you have been gifted with many powers, some Storm and Varick have already shown you, but others you are still unaware of. It is those powers we now have need of, we must help you to discover and master them quickly. Sadly, we only have until the next Thunder Moon to prepare you and that is only a short time away", Zi finished.

Zi then started to wave his hands in a circular motion, muttering under his breath when suddenly a book appeared in his hands. Its cover was made up of all the Colors of the rainbow and on it Rebel could just make out the title, "Colors of Flamecore".

"That's the book we have been looking for, Sir, the one that Librarian Zora took", Rebel said in excitement.

"No Rebel, the one that Librarian Zora had was a copy,

this is the original which has always been in my possession. The book in the Peoples Library was only partially complete, I had removed sections of the book in case it ever fell into the wrong hands.

The book you see before you, holds the answers to why Raulf has the dangerous blue aura. It will also help us to defeat Raulf in his challenge for the Key by understanding what the Colors of Flamecore are and how they work", Zi looked at Varick as he said this.

"What do you mean Zi, it was Jonas of the Glaring who made the challenge not Raulf", Varick started to protest.

Zi held up his hand to Varick, "I am sorry my friend,but Jonas was just a front for Raulf. Raulf is seeking more than just the Key, he wants your Crown and the Kingdom. Trust me in this".

Varick was not shocked but was saddened at what he had been told, looking at Zi, "You must guide me, my friend, on what must be done next so that my Queen and my children are released".

Zi nodded and looked at Storm and Shahmaran, "We must work quickly my friends. Raulf, in his ignorance has activated the Chaos Portals. I sensed the first portal being created a short while ago. Raulf has created three portals so far. We must stop the Portals from increasing in number before it is too late".

"What are Chaos Portals and why are they so dangerous?", Rebel asked

"King Varick, do you remember when the Games of

Shengxiao were first held?" Varick nodded at Storm as he spoke to him and replied,

"They were held nearly four hundred years ago when the Gods announced that Twelve Keys to the Heavenly Gates had been made and that only those who were successful in the challenges would receive a Key", Varick recalled the history behind the Kingdom of Shengxiao.

"Yes, you are right, but do you know why the Twelve Keys were created your Majesty?", Varick shook his head, "I am only aware of one purpose for the keys".

Rebel was now looking at Storm with keen interest at what he was about to say.

"The Keys were created for two reasons. The first is that they open the Heavenly Gates. The second most important, and little-known reason is that they have the ability to lock the Chaos Portals.

There are Twelve Keys and Twelve Portals, Raulf has opened three of the portals, and we do not know how. I can only think that his blue aura is getting stronger the more he is underground, it is this I think that has enabled him to open the portals. Before he opens all twelve portals, we must stop him", Storm spoke ominously as he continued speaking,

"If we do not stop the portals from opening, the Kingdom of Shengxiao and all within, will be lost. The Portals are holes in the fabric of this dimension, once all twelve are opened Shengxiao will be lost forever", Storm finished his voice now lowered to a whisper that Rebel could scarcely hear.

At this point Shahmaran hissed impatiently, "ENOUGH,

let us talk about what must be done next we have little time to waste".

"We have twenty-one days before the next Thunder moon and the Games. The only way we can stop Raulf is to make sure he does not get a Key. The only way we can do that is to make sure that a suitable challenger is facing him in the games". Zi looked at Rebel as he spoke.

"Rebel lad, you will be that challenger, only you will be able to defeat him, we will help you develop your magical powers to enable this to happen. Storm, you are in charge of helping Rebel to discover his hidden powers. You have twenty days to do this. Do so, and do so carefully, for even I do not know the strength and ability of Rebel's true powers", said Zi.

"But Jonas is the one who made the challenge, Master Zi... I mean Your Godliness". Rebel stuttered to halt not sure of what to call Zi now that he knew who he was.

"Continue to call me Master Zi, young Rebel, and you are right it was Jonas who made the challenge, but I suspect that he will choose his partner to be Prince Raulf. As part of the Rules for the Games it states challengers' can choose their own partners", with that Zi looked towards Storm and then King Varick.

"Your Majesty, might I suggest that as we still have to announce the games formally, you can choose the challengers to represent the Ratticus family. This way Rebel and Storm can formally stand for them". Zi looked at Varick for his assent and then added...

"Varick my friend, if it is your will, the Caysand Cloak will help Rebel in this challenge as he is of royal blood, he will be able to wear it and use it with ease. Will you allow him to use it?".

"Of course, Zi, if you think it will help, I will do anything to stop Raulf and save the Kingdom from being destroyed", Varick finished with fire in his voice.

Zi nodded with approval continuing, "Varick, Shahmaran and I will go to the Contemplation Hall, we must use the Circle of Time to slow down the Chaos Portals. If we are successful in this, it may give us enough time to stop more of the Chaos Portals from being created. We will need the High Elders from all the Families to be able to do complete this task". Zi then turned to Rebel, "Rebel, please instruct Mercy and Beda to find Drizzle and Crick, we will need their mind meld powers to help us through this, tell them to hurry. Instruct them to reach out to all the High Elders asking them to convene at the Contemplation Hall when the sun is rising on the next day.

Go now all of you and success in your endeavours". Zi then stood up and walked out of the stables with King Varick and Shahmaran.

The sun was just setting in the horizon, the sky was shimmering with the last of the sunshine when Zi stopped in his tracks and looked up. A hint of something ominous was in the air. The others followed his gaze, all could see the night sky approaching with huge clouds rolling towards them dark and foreboding. Varick shivered as a chill went through him.

CHAPTER SEVEN

Rebel could not believe all that had happened in the last day, as he looked at Storm, who now in his eyes, looked so much more than he was before. He just looked larger than life, so powerful and exuded a confidence that Rebel had only glimpsed occasionally before.

"Prince Rebel, what you have learnt changes nothing in our relationship. I am still your mentor in all that you must learn, and we must continue that which we started when we first met", Storm spoke without turning his head to look at Rebel.

"Let us prepare the horses for where we go is a half-day ride from here", Storm turned and chose a grey roan for himself and started to saddle it.

Storm turned to a stable hand who had just appeared and instructed him to go to the kitchens to pack enough food and drink for one week. Within the hour Storm and Rebel were riding out of the palace gates turning as they approached the red trees towards the North. Storm went into a gallop on the open road ahead of him, with Rebel close behind.

"Where are we going?", shouted Rebel, so he could be heard above the sounds of the galloping horses.

"We go to a place few know; it is a place where the Felinia

Black convene. We need their help in getting you ready for the games". Storm then quickened his pace and galloped on ahead with Rebel increasing his pace to match him.

Rebel loved the feel of the wind on his face as he was riding. It brought back memories of his father and himself when they were out on rides together. Rebel revelled in the moment as they left the city far behind on their journey North. Rebel threw his cloak over his shoulders as the wind started to turn chilly the further North they travelled.

It took nearly an hour just to pass the Reds before they even reached the open road. The sun had already set in the west and the night sky was dark with clouds blocking the moonlight. It was now becoming more difficult to navigate the road and Rebel was about to say something, when Storm slowed down to a trot to allow Rebel to come alongside him.

"Rebel lad, it is time to use your night vision, remember I showed you how to use this. We are now approaching the Peak Mountains and to reach our destination within the mountain range, we must ride through the night".

"Yes, Storm I remember, but where are we going?" as he spoke Rebel closed his eyes. After few seconds he opened them again and there was now a visible green tinge around the iris of both eyes, Storm could see that Rebel did indeed remember his lessons well. "Well done lad!". As Rebel looked at Storm he could see that Storm had also turned his night vision on as his eyes also held a green glow.

"We go to a place in the mountains which is hidden from all who look for it. It is called The Valley of the Five, it is a special place where strong flows of energy are present between the different dimensions of existence.

It is here where the Felinia Black learn to understand and master the arts of magic before they go out into the world to find their pupils. I have waited a long time to find you Rebel, I was very glad when you finally started to dream. It was your unconscious mind that called to me.

You would not have been aware of it when you were awake. Only when you slept did your unconscious mind wake. It is this part of you we need to now bring to your waking memories so that you can use this power to defeat Raulf". Storm gave a considering look to Rebel as he finished speaking, then turned his horse giving it a quick dig in the side so it started to trot towards the mountain range ahead.

As they approached the Peak Mountains the ground started to slope gently upwards and was becoming very uneven. The higher they climbed the steeper the path became. Rebel was glad of his night vision as he could guide his horse around the larger stones scattered across the path.

They rode in silence, after a while Storm turned his horse heading towards the trees veering to the right of the path. They had been moving slowly through the forest for about an hour when they came across a small stream where Storm slowed down his mount and stopped.

Storm jumped off his horse and turned to Rebel, "We will leave the horses here Rebel, they do not like The Valley, it makes them jittery. Unsaddle them, and they can roam here close to the water".

Rebel jumped of his horse and followed suit. A short time

later they were making their way through the forest and up the side of the mountain with their packs on their backs. The weather had turned bitterly cold, the air steamed as they breathed heavily with the steep climb upwards.

To Rebel, it felt they had been climbing for hours and just as he was about to ask Storm how much longer it would be, Storm held up his hand motioning him to stop. He then put his finger on his lips to alert Rebel not to say anything.

Storm made a sound which sounded like half growl and half purr. Rebel watched Storm curiously waiting to see what would happen. All of a sudden Rebel found himself standing in a clearing which seemed to have appeared from out of nowhere, Storm stood next to him with a big grin on his face. "Ahhh its good to be back", Storm purred.

Rebel took a few steps back amazed and shocked at the same time, one minute they were in the middle of a forest half-way up the mountain, the next they were standing in the middle of a huge valley. Looking around the valley in wonder, he started to feel a tingling all over his body, which usually only happened when magic was around him. Nudging Storm in warning, Rebel went into a defensive position not knowing what to expect.

Rebel's mind went on high alert as the unusual feeling coursed through him, his thoughts started to race through his mind at an extraordinarily fast pace. It was as if he could feel himself finally waking up out of a dream and suddenly becoming aware of the world around him. All his senses became heightened, and he looked at Storm in amazement.

Storm looked back at him with a grin on his face, "Good

you have become aware of the Quincunxes without any help, that was the first step. I was hopeful that you would be able to do this on your own. Come Rebel we will rest first and then start work at first light which by the looks of it is fast approaching", he turned quickly towards a Felinia Black who had suddenly appeared in front of them.

Again, Rebel stepped back with a start, far too many surprises were happening too quickly for his liking, it was making him feel extremely uncomfortable. However, Storm again just grinned and slapped Rebel gently on the shoulder.

"Greetings Katrina, I have missed you. Rebel meet my Queen, Katrina, she will show you to your quarters where you can freshen up and rest for a few hours". With that Storm then grabbed Katrina and kissed her passionately before letting her go.

Rebel looked at Storm agog at what was happening in front of him, the Storm he knew was not the Storm he saw before him. It was if he had been friends with a totally different person. Looking at the two of them together Rebel could see they were very much in love.

Queen Katrina was a lot smaller than Storm by at least a foot and half, she was also a very buxom woman with hair that was a mixture of white and black cropped short and eyes that glowed blue. Rebel knew by looking at her she was a pure-bred Felinia by the Intensity of the colour of her eyes. Rebel was mesmerised by Katrina.

"Hahahaha", Storm laughed out loud... "you've done it again dear, captured another young heart. Beautiful isn't she Rebel?". He looked at Rebel with a sly grin on his face.

“Be aware Rebel, Katrina is a very talented Felinia Black, she will be helping me to teach you over the next few days. So, I strongly suggest you go and get some rest now as you may not get to rest again for a while if Katrina has anything to do with it”.

With that Storm turned, holding Katrina’s hand they walked away. Rebel could hear Storm chuckling at something Katrina had said and smiled to himself. He liked this Storm so much more. They headed towards some tents that had been set up on one side of the huge clearing, Rebel following behind slowly, bemused at what Storm had just said, he was looking forward to a few hours rest as he realised how much his muscles were aching after their long journey from the Kingdom.

Sophia didn’t know where they were going, she was totally disorientated by the tunnels and had started to feel a little claustrophobic. She could feel the dragon in her waking up as the situation became more stressful. She consciously slowed her breathing, trying to keep calm to contain her dragon self.

Sophia thought back to what had transpired before Raulf had come to get her. Zi to her utter surprise, had opened a magical rift from the Royal Stables. This rift had allowed Zi to communicate with Sophia in the room she had been imprisoned with her mother. He had explained that the rift only allowed communication and it was imperative that he find out what Raulf had discovered about the Colors of Flamecore.

At the time she was not aware that Raulf knew anything, Zi had quickly explained that plans were in motion to rescue them and to find a way to defeat Raulf. He had also told Sophia that Raulf was getting more powerful the longer he remained underground in the tunnels and to be incredibly careful around him and definitely not to antagonise him.

It was directly linked he said to the knowledge contained in the book "The Colors of Flamecore". Zi carefully, explained to Sophia her role in aiding them to defeat Raulf to protect the Kingdom. Matters were now even more grave than originally thought explained Zi. Zi finished the conversation with a quick wave goodbye and closed the rift.

Queen Althea was totally unaware of what had happened as Zi had stopped time while the rift was open. The Queen had been held in a time warp as he and Sophia talked. Sophia did not enlighten her as instructed by Zi.

Just as Zi had closed the rift between them Raulf walked in. Sophia could see that Raulf had wrinkled his nose as he entered the room, and she realised that the smell lingering in the room had come from the Royal Stables when Zi had opened the rift.

Sophia was brought back from her thoughts to the present as Nagid spoke suddenly, "Prince Raulf we will enter the Forbidden Steps shortly. Are you certain you want to down them?", Nagid looked fearfully at Raulf as he spoke.

Sophia was not sure if Nagid was fearful of the Forbidden Steps or Raulf, deciding it was probably both. She remained silent watching Raulf for his response. Raulf had changed a lot in the short time they had been in the Nest and looking at him, Sophia was scared too, more so now, as she scarcely recognised her brother realising that being underground with the Flamecore close by was having a huge effect upon him. She kept her face expressionless as she watched the altercation between the two.

“It is not a choice Nagid, I must enter Flamecore, the only way in is by going down the Forbidden Steps. But before we do I must speak with Sophia as she is the only one who can help me to attain the power of the Flamecore”. Raulf looked at Sophia as he spoke pulling her into a small alcove to the right of the entrance to the Forbidden Steps.

“Sister dear, like you I now also have the knowledge of our ancestors thanks to the Flamecore. That knowledge has made me aware that you know the magical mantra to the Forbidden Steps. So, do not try to trick me by saying the wrong words as we make our way down the Steps, as I also know the consequences of you doing that. Is that clear?”.

“How do you know that I know the words Raulf?”. Sophia was stalling trying to remember exactly what Zi had told her she must do.

The magical mantra to the Forbidden Steps could be used in two ways Zi had explained. The first would allow the person who used the words, to correctly descend the Steps and enter the chamber of the Flamecore safely.

The second was to change the first and last word of the seven magical words of the mantra and the Forbidden Steps would take them to another chamber which was a false chamber holding a mirror image of the Flamecore.

This was a time warp room and every time someone tried to take the Flamecore, they would find themselves at the top of the Forbidden Steps again. This time loop would continue until the correct sequence of words was used. She recalled Zi's final words, "Be aware Princess that you can only loop one hundred times, after which you will be held for eternity". Sophia shivered at the thought of being stuck with Raulf for all eternity.

Raulf grabbed her arm and pulled her towards the Forbidden Steps, looking at Nagid Raulf said, "Wait here for us to return Nagid, we should not be long". With that he pushed Sofia forward to the first step and instructed her to start the magical mantra.

Sofia gasped as Raulf squeezed her arm painfully, "Let me go Raulf, I need time to think, I must say them correctly for the Forbidden Steps to allow us entry". With that Sophia pulled her arm free from Raulf's grasp rubbing it to ease the pain.

Sofia repeated the correct mantra in her mind, "Forbidden Flamecore Lets All Men Enter Steps"

Then Sofia repeated it again just like Zi had instructed her, "Steps Flamecore Lets All Men Enter Forbidden".

Sofia repeated it a number of times before she turned to Raulf with an outward confidence she did not feel. "I am ready, but I want you to release mother Raulf, before I will do this. She is not coping well-being held in that room". Sofia met Raulf's eyes as she said this and stared at him without wavering. Inside Sofia was quaking with fear and hoped that it didn't show.

Raulf stared back at his sister and saw her resolve, then turned towards Nagid, "Nagid once we have entered the

Steps release my mother". As he finished speaking, he looked pointedly at Sofia. "Your turn sister".

Sofia took a deep breath turning towards the Steps, "Remember Raulf, once I have started the Magic Mantra you must take each step at the same time as I do, otherwise only I will enter". Sofia then turned to face the steps as Raulf stood beside her grabbing her arm, "This will make sure that we take the steps together", he said ominously.

Sofia did not look at him, taking a deep breath she said the first word and then took the first step down, "STEPS…", with the utterance of the first word they disappeared from sight. The Forbidden Steps had now become invisible to anyone who was watching.

Nagid looked on fearfully, as Raulf and Sofia took the first step, then as they vanished from sight. He breathed a sigh of relief to finally be away from Raulf. Nagid had lived in fear of his life since he had mistakenly agreed to help Raulf. When he had tried to take back his offer of help Raulf had threatened Nagid's family. Nagid had first-hand experience of the pain that Raulf could inflict, because of this he had now become an unwilling accomplice to Raulf.

Nagid quickly made his way back to where Queen Althea was being held and opened the door to her room. Queen Althea was asleep on the bed. Nagid made his way to the side of the bed and gently shook her to wake her up.

"Your Majesty I have been instructed to release you, please hurry. I'm sorry for everything my Queen, please please hurry", Nagid was so scared he was lisping and hissing at the same time.

Althea woke up disorientated and only caught some of what Nagid was saying.

"What did you say, I cannot understand you, slow down and stop hissing at me", Althea commanded angrily.

Nagid looked at her fearfully and slowly repeated himself, "Your Majesty, Raulf has ordered me to release you, please hurry".

"What about Sofia and Jai? I cannot leave without them", Sofia stood up from the bed and straightened her clothes as she did so.

"Your Majesty I was not instructed to release Prince Jai, and Sofia has entered the Forbidden Steps with Raulf", Nagid had started to transform as much as he tried not to, but the stress always made him change to his animal form. His last words before he changed were, "please follow me quickly Majessssstyyy".

With that Nagid slithered towards the exit of the door only stopping to raise his head, to indicate to the Queen to follow him. Queen Althea had no choice but to follow, within the hour she was stood outside alone and disorientated near the cluster of trees half-way down the Mound.

Althea took a deep breath and looked around the area. When she finally got her bearings she hitched up her dress and quickly started to make her way up towards the top of the Mound not sure what day or time it was as it was still dark, but unlike the night she had been abducted, the moon was now hidden by ominous looking dark clouds.

CHAPTER EIGHT

Zi, King Varick and Shahmaran made their way quickly to the Contemplation Hall where some of the High Elders had already gathered. As they entered the room the aroma of freshly baked bread and roasted meats assailed their nostrils, and their stomachs grumbled noisily.

Zi turned to his companions, "We should all eat something while we wait for the others to arrive. I don't know about you but I haven't eaten since yesterday and if we are to succeed in our task we must have the energy to do so". Zi then made his way to the tables laden with food and started to pile his plate high with the sumptuous food before him.

Varick hesitated, the very thought of eating while his family was missing was unpalatable.

"I know you may not wish to eat Your Majesty but eat you must. Energy is needed for the task ahead if we are to achieve the impossible", Shahmaran lisped the words quietly into his ear and gave him a gentle nudge towards the food. Varick knew she was right and reluctantly moved towards the tables.

As they were eating High Elders of the different families started to arrive, some together, some alone. By the time Ziand his companions had finished eating all had arrived including the twins Dribble and Crick as well as Mercy and Beda.

As before Zi instructed Mercy and Beda to stand outside the doors of the Contemplation Hall with instructions to let nobody in under any circumstances. He also asked Beda to inform the Kings Guard to close and protect the Palace Gates. Both acknowledged their instructions leaving quickly and closing the doors of the Contemplation Hall behind them.

Zi then turned towards everyone in the room, holding up his hands he motioned to everyone to stop speaking.

"What happened at the annual Shengxiao Games is unprecedented". As Zi spoke he transformed himself into Tai Sui. The sound of loud gasps and exclamations of awe echoed around the room at what they were witnessing.

"Because of this I now stand before you in my true form, Tai Sui, God of Age". Zi's voice now boomed across the room as he had grown at least another six feet taller and was now towering above everyone in the room. Zi continued to speak, "What we are about to do now has never been done before, and I hope we will never have to do again. We will stop the Circle of Time so that we can prevent Prince Raulf from opening the Chaos Portals. The only way we can do this is by having all twelve High Elders present. We know that the Ratticus family do not have a High Elder presently so until the next full moon when the games will be played, we need a proxy.

That proxy will be Dribble". Dribble looked at Zi in surprise as he heard his name.

"There are two reasons I choose you Dribble, one you are from the Ratticus Family, and two you can mind meld with your brother Crick. The latter being the most important for this task".

Turning to Varick, Zi instructed him and Dribble to go to an antechamber in the Contemplation Hall to perform the High Elder Ceremony giving Dribble the new Ratticus Key to the Heavenly Gates. "Do not take long Varick, time is of the essence", finished Zi.

To the others gathered in the room Zi instructed them to sit within the Circle of Time. Each section was a different colour with one section allocated to each family. At the edge of the outer circle the family animal was encircled. They all sat on top of their family animal.

All sections flowed to the centre of the Circle of Time where another Circle had been placed. This circle was a meld of all the colours and animals. Before their very eyes the central circle began to rise upwards until it was three feet above the ground. Zi made his way to the central circle and sat upon it.

Just then King Varick and Dribble came into the room, Zi instructed them both to sit at their relevant sections on the Circle of Time.

He then turned to Crick, "Crick you will be critical in ensuring the success of the task ahead of us. You must convey to all, the instructions I will speak in my mind simultaneously. Dribble will aid you in this task. Dribble conveys to the five High Elders immediately to your left. Crick to the remaining six. We must all say the instructions and use the Keys as instructed at the same time for us to stop the Circle of Time". Zi paused and looked at all of them to ensure they had understood the gravity of what he was saying.

Zi continued once he saw that all had acknowledged their understanding of the instructions he had given. "Once we have completed the task you must all stay in your positions for three days. That is the longest we can stop the Circle of Time without causing severe time warps in this dimension".

Turning to Crick, "Crick once the last instruction is given, we will become invisible in this dimension. Once that happens you are to send messages to Rebel and Storm instructing them of what has taken place, and that they must be ready to meet us back here in the Contemplation Hall in three days' time. This is earlier than they expected, however, they must meet here before the sun sets on the third day!".

Crick nodded and bowed low to Zi, "Master Zi, I will do as you bid". Crick then went to stand directly behind Dribble and placed his hands on his brothers' shoulders in readiness of the task ahead of him.

Zi sat cross-legged on the platform and closed his eyes, instructing all within the circle to do the same and then to place their hands directly in front of them making sure that their palms were face down flat on the surface of the circle.

As soon as they all had their hands in position, the keywords engraved in the circles started to glow. A mirror image of each of the keywords glowed brightly just six inches above the ground where each word was engraved.

"Crick and Drizzle, we do not have a lot of time, repeat after me and relay this information to the others accurately and simultaneously", Zi instructed telepathically. Both

Crick and Drizzle acknowledged Zi with a mental assent.

"High Elders we are about to create a time loop so that we may halt time. Please note that you MUST all repeat the words out loud that you will hear Drizzle and Crick reveal to you in your minds. It is imperative that you repeat immediately after the words have been spoken for this to work. As you say the words that are pertinent to you please use your Keys as you have been shown. Once you have done this place both hands back onto the floor palms down on either side of the word. Are you all ready to begin?"

Drizzle and Crick had relayed all the instructions to the Twelve High Elders', and all gave their mental acknowledgements.

Zi took a deep breath and started to speak, with Drizzle and Crick repeating what he was saying immediately after each word spoken.

First Ratticus element Water
Second Oxbow element Earth
Third Panthera element Wood
Fourth Leporidae element Wood
Fifth Dragnonian element Earth
Sixth Serpentes element Fire
Seventh Equidae element Fire
Eighth Bovidae element Earth
Ninth Simian element Metal
Tenth Gallus element Metal
Eleventh Canis element Earth
Twelfth Suidae element Water

As Zi spoke each line the High Elders of each family

spoke the words out loud and used their keys as they had been shown by King Varick, they then each placed their palms face down on either side of the engraved word. When the twelfth key had been used the keywords started to dim in brightness.

Zi then spoke one word loudly, "REVERSE". The words started to rotate anti-clockwise slowly at first and then within seconds they moved so fast that all you could see was a circle of light. As soon as that happened all within the Circle of Time vanished. Crick was left standing there alone and a little afraid. Quickly remembering Zi's instructions Crick sent a mind message to Storm. "Storm can you hear me. Storm? Storm?" Crick was literally shouting Storm's name when Storm shouted back, "Yes, loud and clear stop shouting you're giving me a headache. What is it friend is all well with you?" Crick relayed what had transpired so quickly that he was tripping over his words. Storm had to ask him to repeat the instructions a number of times so that he understood it fully. Finally, once Storm understood what was required, he gave a mental nod and said.

"I understand Crick, Rebel and I will be there at the given time, take care my friend". Storm acknowledged and left Crick's mind.

Storm opened his eyes and looked directly at Rebel who was sat facing him at the breakfast table. "Rebel lad we have only three days to complete your training as the situation back at the Kingdom is getting worse".

Looking at Katrina Storm stated, "Kat you have less than three days to get Rebel ready. We must leave at noon on the third day to get back to the Palace. Do what you do best Kat, the Kingdom depends on it". Storm finished as he stood up and walked out of the tent. Kat acknowledged Storm's request by turning to Rebel

"Okay Rebel let us get started, come with me we have a lot to cover over the next few days". Kat led Rebel out and made her way across to a tent at the far side of the field.

As Rebel followed, he could not believe the thoughts running through his mind, it was if a whole new world of knowledge had opened up to him, and he couldn't wait to try some of these new-found skills.

They were nearly at the tent when Rebel stopped suddenly and fell to his knees, "Katrina, someone is trying to talk to me", gasped Rebel.

Katrina turned around and quickly going to her knees and grasped Rebel's hands palm to palm. "Rebel I can help you to listen to the voice more clearly, hold tightly and focus on the voice only".

Rebel opened his eyes wide as he realised that Katrina was also speaking to him in his mind. "Close your eyes Rebel lad and focus", Katrina coached him.

"If you can hear me its Prince Jai, please acknowledge if you can hear me, I can hear you somehow your thoughts invaded mine so you should be able to hear me. Who is this, is it Rebel?", Jai kept repeating the same thing, again and again.

"My Prince I can hear you, yes its Rebel, how are you able to do this?"

"I'm not sure how I can do this with you. Your thoughts suddenly invaded my mind a few hours ago. You must help me Rebel, I am being held in the Serpentes Nest. All my dragon senses have gone on high alert since I have been here. I am struggling to keep my human form. I cannot change as the room I am being held is too small and it will kill me if I change into my dragon. I'm not sure how much longer I can keep the change at bay". Rebel could sense that Prince Jai was struggling to speak as his voice switched from human to dragon every other sentence.

"Your Highness, this is Katrina of the Felinia Black, I can send someone to you, but it will take a couple of days. In the meantime, I can help you to remain in your human form if you allow me your Highness". Katrina spoke calmly and firmly.

"Yes, Katrina I know of you, please do whatever you can to help me. Something down here is heightening my abilities and the transition to dragon is getting harder to control as it is more powerful than my human self", Jai spoke quickly.

"Close your eyes Highness and focus on your human form, I am going to flick the switch in your mind that will stop your dragon from forming". Katrina closed her eyes and a few seconds later she spoke,

"It is done Highness; you should have no problems in controlling it now until help can get to you. Can you give us any clues as to where in the Nest you are being held?" asked Katrina.

"No sorry, the tunnels are so vast I have no idea, and mother and Sophia are being held in another room somewhere else in the Nest. Can you tell me what is happening

Rebel?" Jai asked of Rebel.

"Know this Prince Jai, we are doing everything we can to find you all. Prince Raulf has made a challenge for one of the Twelve Keys and the Kingdom is in turmoil". Rebel was relaying all this information when Katrina interrupted, "I'm sorry highness we are short of time we must go now. I will be in touch with you as soon as I have made arrangements for someone to come to you", finished Katrina quickly as she broke the connection. Rebel opened his eyes and exclaimed. "What happened! How could I do that? I have never been able to do that before!" "Rebel your powers are far beyond what even I could have imagined, I don't think we will have any problems getting you ready in the short time that we have been given", Katrina said looking at Rebel in amazement.

"As I entered your mind, I could feel an enormous amount of power emanating from the deepest regions of your brain. Once this is unlocked you are going to become a very powerful individual with unfathomable magical powers. I hope you are ready to cope with this. I will help you as much as I can Rebel", said Katrina standing up.

"Let us make our way to the middle of the field as your first lesson will involve the mastering of the five Elements, water, earth, wood, fire and metal", Katrina turned and started walking towards the middle of the field as she was talking with Rebel keeping pace beside her.

"The first element we will work on is Earth", spoke Katrina when they had reached what was roughly the middle of the field. Katrina sat down cross-legged and motioned Rebel to do the same. Placing her hands in Rebel's, Katrina closed her eyes and Rebel felt her enter his mind.

"Rebel clear your mind of all thoughts and focus only on the Element Earth. Once you have done this, I want you to imagine creating an object with the earth. I am going to leave your mind now and as soon as you feel I have gone, start", as soon as Katrina had finished she opened her eyes and to her amazement just behind Rebel a lifelike statue of Mercy stood made from the earth.

"Open your eyes Rebel and look behind you", Katrina whispered.

"But I haven't done what you asked of me", Rebel complained.

"Look behind you Rebel", Katrina spoke more firmly. Rebel opened his eyes, turned and looked behind him and gasped out loud.

"What the.... how did that happen?", Rebel spoke with amazement in his voice.

"You did that Rebel and I've seen nothing of the like before. Okay close your eyes and try it again", instructed Katrina.

Rebel closed his eyes and within minutes the field was covered with images of people, animals and other objects that Rebel was obviously thinking about including an image of Storm and Katrina kissing, the last one made Katrina smile, tapping Rebel on the arm and instructing him to open his eyes.

Rebel looked around in amazement with a huge grin on his face as he looked at Katrina. "I think I have this element in the bag", he said with a cheeky wink at Katrina.

Katrina smiled at Rebel and then instructed him with the next lesson... "This time Rebel I need you to focus your mind on specific objects and change them into the Element of Metal. To do this, you must isolate an object and then think of how you can change it from the Element Earth to the Element Metal".

Rebel closed his eyes and like the last time it took him only seconds to change objects from Earth to Metal. This time, however, he also started to shape some from the Element Water to Katrina's amazement he had achieved all of this in a blink of the eye.

Katrina looked at Rebel in wonder, "Rebel I don't think it will take us three days to get you ready I have never in all my years seen anyone do what you can with just a thought. Your magical ability is beyond anyone's I have ever seen" and as Katrina was speaking she looked around in amazement as Rebel was now changing objects from Earth to Water to Metal instantly and doing so without closing his eyes, but just looking at Katrina with a huge grin as he did so.

Rebel shifted his gaze from Katrina's face to look behind her and then back at her, motioning her to turn around with his eyes. Katrina turned slowly to see what he was looking at and gasped at what she saw. Rebel had uprooted a tree and it was floating to where they stood. As it reached them the tree started to rotate slowly as it rotated Rebel started to shape the tree. After a few minutes, the tree stopped rotating and lowered to the ground.

Katrina clasped her hands to her face and gasped staring wide-eyed. There in front of her was a lifelike statue of King Varick carved out of the tree.

From behind, another tree was hovering above the ground and Rebel had shaped this into Varick's dragon. "Watch closely Katrina", spoke Rebel with a whisper.

The dragon started to move and opened its' mouth, a loud noise emanated from its mouth and flames appeared to shoot out for a distance of over five feet.

Katrina fell backwards to the ground in shock and amazement "How, howwww did you do that?", she gasped. Rebel had mastered all five Elements within a short space of time. Katrina was in shock.

"I don't know but it was easy I just think about what I want, and it just happens", spoke Rebel with a slight quiver in his voice. "I'm a little dazed, my mind is so full of wonderous and new knowledge, I don't know where to start and what to do with it".

Katrina pushed herself up from the ground and brushed the dirt from her clothes as she did so, shock mirrored on her face, her mind was full of confusion at what she had witnessed. Never in all her years had she witnessed anything like it before.

Katrina spoke slowly to Rebel a quiver in her voice, "I think Rebel that your power is far beyond what I can teach you. You will need somebody more powerful than me and the only person I can think of who can fulfil this role is Zi. What I can teach you is how to harness your power once you are out of the Valley of the Five. We can do this part in the warmth of our tent, let us go". Katrina instructed as she walked away purposefully. This time however, she had to walk around all the objects that Rebel had created. Katrina shouted back at Rebel, "Oh and please get rid of these otherwise the horses will have nowhere to graze", she said with a twinkle in her eye.

Rebel smiled back and suddenly everything around them collapsed and disappeared back into the ground. "I think we can leave the two wooden statues of King Varick as a memento Katrina, what do you think?" laughed Rebel as he followed Katrina back to the tent.

CHAPTER NINE

"What did you do Sofia?", Raulf shouted frustratedly as they were back on the top step for the twenty-fourth time. Every time they descended the steps and took a step into the room holding the "Flamecore" they would find themselves back at the top of the steps.

"You tricked me, you will live to regret this sister", Raulf screamed in anger at Sofia and going bright red in the face as he did so, his veins bulging in his forehead.

Sofia did not flinch knowing that there was little he could do. Only she could break the spell as she was the one who had uttered the first spell. Sofia looked at Raulf with contempt, "Did you really think I would let you get hold of the "Flamecore", Raulf? Never, never would I betray our father like you have done, or my people you arrogant pig", Sofia literally spat out the words as they continued to descend the steps again for the twenty-fifth time.

Sofia recalled that Zi had told her the cycle would continue for one hundred cycles, at which time they could either break the spell or they would be held forever within the steps. Sofia had to break the spell at ninety-nine as that would give enough time for Zi to do what he needed to stop the Circle of Time.

Once Zi had achieved this, Raulf would be unable to open

any more portals and thus taking the Kingdom out of imminent danger.

Sofia was making a mental note of the number of times they had repeated the cycle so that she didn't accidentally go over one hundred. She shivered with the thought of being trapped within the time loop of the Steps with Raulf. Blocking out his whining, Sofia continued to keep careful count of the number of loops they had done.

Tap, tap, tap… tap, tap, tap… Prince Jai stood up from where he was sat and made his way towards the door where the tapping was coming from. "Who goes there? Jai whispered, tap, tap, tap. "Who goes there?" Jai spoke a little louder.

"Your Highness it's Keon of the Oxbow Herd, I have Crick with me too. Please stand back as I am going to break the door down". Prince Jai moved to the opposite side of the room and crouched down quickly.

Suddenly, there was a couple of loud smacks from what sounded like a hammer and the door flew off its hinges landing just a few feet from Jai.

Jai jumped up and walked quickly towards the now doorless entrance and gratefully slapped Keon on the back. "How did you know where to find me?" said Jai looking at both Crick and Keon, when he noticed that a Serpentes Royal Guard was stood close by.

"Crick had received a mind-meld message from someone called Katrina to find a way into the Nest to free you as you were being held prisoner. We asked Royal Guard Asp who is loyal to the King to show us the way in", Keon finished with a whisper.

“Wait, we must also free my mother and sister”, Jai spoke with an authority that made everyone standstill. “Highness, the Queen is free and at the Palace already, we believe that your sister Princess Sofia has trapped herself and Prince Raulf in a time loop on the Forbidden Steps at the instructions of Master Zi”.

“Master Zi? What does he have to do with all this?”, Jai asked puzzled.

“Highness let us get out of here quickly before we are discovered”. “We can answer your questions once we are out”, whispered Crick as he started to make his way up the tunnel behind Royal Guard Asp.

They all made their way quietly and quickly through the tunnels. After nearly forty minutes they approached one of the exits to the Nest. Asp held up his hand to slow everyone down and slowly made his way to the exit transforming into his snake form as he did so. He slithered quietly out of the entrance. The others waited quietly, crouching down so that they were less visible to anyone coming down the tunnels.

After about ten minutes Royal Guard Asp walked back into the tunnel, this time in his human form. Whispering, “All issss clear let us go now before anyone comessss”.He then turned and led them all to the outside and freedom.

Jai breathed in deeply as he stepped outside, he had missed the fresh air so much he realised and grinned widely at his rescuers, before becoming more serious. “Let us go to the palace straight away we have no time to waste”, Jai ordered.

Crick led the way down the mound to the horses that were tethered to a tree. "We brought your mount Highness". Crick looked at Jai as he handed him the reigns of his horse before climbing atop his own horse. Jai acknowledged with a small smile as he mounted his horse and set off on a quick trot.

As they made their way towards the Palace, Crick rode alongside the Prince and filled him in on what had transpired since he had been taken captive nearly a week ago. The more Jai listened to Crick, the angrier he became at Raulf.

"How could he do this to us?", Jai spoke angrily to no one in particular before going into silent contemplation about the whole situation.

Crick quickly glanced towards him and saw that Jai was deep in thought, unconsciously he had also nudged his horse to a canter and started to lean forward encouraging his horse into a faster gallop. The others followed suit and soon they were far away from the Serpentes Nest as they made their way towards the Palace.

Storm, Rebel and Katrina were sitting at a table in their tent looking at each other, all at a loss for words. When Rebel suddenly spoke. "I don't know what the big deal is, so I did the tasks faster than you expected. It just means we can go back to the Kingdom that much earlier", Rebel finished looking at both Storm and Katrina with a twinkle in his eye.

"Rebel, Rebel… I... ah... err… Storm!" Katrina started to say and then stopped shaking her head and looked at Storm to help her out.

"I think what Katrina is trying to say Rebel, is that it's

not only a big deal it's just unfathomable what you have achieved, and she is at a loss as to how to deal with you". "Am I correct in my assumption Katrina dear?" Katrina nodded and looked at Rebel again with wonder on her face.

"Never, never have I seen the like before Rebel, in all my centuries I have never come across anyone with the ability you have. Special that's what you are, Special", Katrina finished.

"Well while you were gone, I received a message from Crick. Raulf has been opening Chaos Portals without realising the danger he is putting the Kingdom into. Zi with the Twelve High Elders have decided to stop the Circle of Time to prevent Raulf opening any more". Storm took a gulp of milk from his tankard as he finished speaking wiping a dribble of his chin looking at Rebel as he did so.

An expression of realisation flitted across Storm's face, and he turned towards Katrina, "My dear get the horses ready we ride today to the Kingdom, I think I know how Rebel and I can win the games and therefore the Key", Storm purred with delight as he saw confusion reflected on both Katrina and Rebels faces.

"Don't worry all will be explained, and all will become clear soon enough. Now let us get ready to leave within the hour please". Storm stood up from the table grabbing histankard as he did so. With two huge gulps he finished his drink and ushered them both out of the tent.

An hour later they were all mounted and making their way out of The Valley of the Five. As they approached the barrier, which was now visible to Rebel with his newly found powers, Rebel slowed and stopped his horse.

Looking at Katrina he said, “What If I lose my power once I leave the Valley?” Rebel spoke will a little trepidation in his voice.

“You will not lose it Rebel, that is the beauty of the magic of the Valley. It has opened up your mind, and your power, it is yours and only yours to master. The Quincunxes help those with magic to fully utilise their abilities. It helps them to open their minds to their potential and once open it cannot be closed unless you want it to be closed”. Katrina looked at Rebel with a smile on her face. “I think Rebel, you are going to become one of the greatest magicians the Kingdom of Shengxiao has ever known, maybe even the world has ever seen”, Katrina nodded to Storm to continue, and they all made their way slowly through the barrier of the Valley of the Five.

The gates of the Palace were closed, and Royal Guards were posted at the front the gates, stopping all those who wanted to enter. As Prince Jai approached, the Royal Guard stood to attention as they recognised Prince Jai.

“Open the gatesss for hisss Royal Highnessss Prince Jai”, Royal Guard Asp shouted as they came to a halt in front of the gates.

“I’m sorry my Prince”, one of the guards replied, “We cannot by order of the King, the gates must stay closed until the order is given by the King himself to reopen them”.

“Open the gates man”, shouted Keon, “Can you not see it is his Royal Highness Prince Jai?”

“We are truly sorry sir, but the Kings orders cannot be changed by anyone but the King”, the Guard finished looking a little scared as Keon was quite frightening to look at when he became angry.

“Where is my mother the Queen?” Jai said ominously looking at the Guard.

“Highness, the Queen has made her way to the People’s Library as we could not allow her entry either”. This time the guard looked down at his feet too afraid to look at Prince Jai directly as he spoke.

“Let us go to the People’s Library then”, instructed Jai turning his horse as he spoke and galloped away from the Palace, not looking back to see if the others were following.

As they rode up to the entrance of the People’s Library, Jai jumped of his horse and ran in shouting, “Mother, mother, where is my mother?” to no one in particular.

From the Pillar of the First Trine Librarian Xin came hurrying out with the Queen one step behind him.

Queen Althea flung herself into her sons’ arms sobbing as she did so. “Mother, mother, Are you okay? Did he hurt you? I’ll kill him when I find him for what he has done to us”. Jai spat the words out in anger as he looked at his mother, who now looked so frail he was scared she would snap in his arms if he held her too tightly.

“No, no, Jai I am okay my dear. They took Sophia and I don’t know what has become of her or your father”, sobbed the Queen.

"Your Majesty, perhaps you would like to come back to my quarters and rest", Librarian Xin spoke calmly, and as he did so he ushered them all towards the entrance of the First Trine towards his private quarters away from the whispering crowd that had started to gather.

Once in his quarters Librarian Xin poured them all a small drink of whiskey-fire a popular drink among the Dragonians. Prince Jai swallowed his in one gulp and then poured himself another. As he did so, he turned towards Crick instructing him to repeat again what had transpired after he, his mother and sister had been abducted.

Once Crick had repeated it all again, Jai turned towards Librarian Xin asking him to relay what had transpired at the Peoples Library. As he was finishing Jai interrupted him, "Who has the cloak now Librarian Xin?"

"Your Highness, the one called Storm gave it a girl called Mercy and they both left for the Palace with it", Xin finished calmly. "I think Storm knew what it was as he had an expression of surprise on his face when he picked it up. It seemed as though he recognised it!"

"Keon and Asp, please stay here and guard the Queen, make sure no harm comes to her", Prince Jai commanded. "Librarian Xin please take me to a private room where I will not be disturbed. Crick you will accompany us!".

"Please follow me your Highness", acknowledged Xin as he made his way out. Xin headed down the stairs from his quarters back into the main library. Wending his way through the various aisles of bookshelves he finally came to a stop in front of a section of books marked the Family Tree of the Dragonian Clan.

Looking around quickly Xin made sure no one else was watching as he lowered himself down to the bottom shelf, where there were a number of multicoloured books. No one book was the same colour and Jai and Crick watched on as Librarian Xin depressed two books simultaneously. One book was green the other yellow, as he did so a mechanism could be heard clicking.... click, click, click, click. At the fourth click the whole bookshelf slid to the right and revealed a secret entrance to a hidden room.

"Quickly your Highness, this way", Librarian Xin ushered both Jai and Crick into the room. As he himself entered, he pulled down a lever jutting from the wall to his right, the bookshelf slowly slid back into place behind him.

Jai looked around him in amazement, the room was dimly lit, a blazing fire burned in an open hearth to one side of the room, making it warm and welcoming. The other three walls were filled with books of every description, size and colour.

"What is this place?", Crick spoke softly.

"No one can hear us here Crick, you do not need to whisper", Librarian Xin smiled at Crick as he spoke, "This room holds the tomes of ancient magic that belonged to the Dragonian Clan. Princess Sofia spent a lot of time in here trying to find out more about Prince Raulf's blue aura by the order of the King".

"Only those who wield magic can enter this room", finished Xin cryptically.

“Then that means you also have magic of some kind Librarian Xin?”, Jai asked looking at Xin directly.

“I do Your Highness”, Xin replied saying no more but stood staring at Jai and then Crick.

“What is your magic Xin?”, Crick asked impatiently

“I am the holder of all the knowledge contained within these books, however I can only answer to specific questions you ask. I am unable to suggest anything to you, Your Majesty”, Xin finished speaking and as he did so he turned and stared at one book in particular.

Jai and Crick followed his gaze not quite sure which book he was looking at. Crick made his way across to the wall of books Xin was staring at and said, “Xin please tell me the name of the book you are looking at”.

“The book is called “The Dragon Games”, Xin replied still looking at the book in question.

Prince Jai had also made his way across to the bookshelf and was reaching to get the book in question, which was on the second to top shelf. Unable to grab it he looked around for a step of some kind and spotted a small wooden stool next to the fireplace. Getting it quickly he stood on the stool and lifted the book down. Jai made his way to a small table with two chairs situated in the middle of the room and sat down.

“Librarian Xin please take a seat and tell me the content of this book and why it is relevant to our situation now?” Jai spoke opening the book with extreme care as it looked as though it was hundreds of years old judging by the condition of the book.

"Prince Jai the Dragon Games were the first-ever games played in the Kingdom before the Gods decided to hold the Shengxiao Games. The Dragon Games formed the basis of the games as they are now but with one big difference", Xin paused and looked at Crick and then Jai.

Taking a deep breath Xin continued, "Currently the games are played using the Five Earthly Elements, Earth, Water, Metal, Wood and Fire", …

"Yes, yes man we know that tell us something we don't know", Crick butted in impatiently.

Xin looked at Crick with a frown on his face when Prince Jai turned to Crick and said, "Silence Crick allow Librarian Xin to speak"

"Highness, as I was saying the current games are played using the Five Earthly Elements, the Dragon Games, however, were more physical, using brute strength and willpower to overcome their opponents. With the Dragon Games, death of your opponents was the way of achieving dominance and power over the clan.

When the Shengxiao games were introduced by the Gods, fighting to the death was banned as it was causing too much friction and malice among the Dragon Clans", Xin went silent and stared at the Prince questioningly.

Jai looked at him, a frown marring his features, "Continue man!", he exclaimed.

Xin remained silent looking now at Crick. It suddenly dawned on Crick that they had to ask him another question as Xin's magic kept him silent.

"Oh, oh a question Highness is what we need to ask of Xin for him to continue", Crick said quickly "Errm Librarian Xin, please tell us how this will help us in winning the Key from Raulf at the games?". Crick finished peering at Xin.

Unbeknown to Xin and Prince Jai, Crick had been trying to read Xin's mind since he had discovered that Xin had this special magical skill. However, no matter what he tried he could not read his mind. It was if there was nothing there just a blank space and Crick knew this was not right.

"There is a clause within the rules of the Shengxiao Games which allows only the ruling King to revert the games back to the way they were played originally. By reverting the games back to The Dragon Games, only the Dragonian Clans can take part which means that the other eleven families do not have to take part. It will also mean that the only available Key will now be the one belonging to the Dragonians. The Ratticus Family will keep their Key. Therefore, in so doing we can minimise the damage to the Kingdom", finished Xin with a flourish and huge grin on his face as he looked first at Crick and then Prince Jai. The grin faded from his face as he looked at the expression on Prince Jai's face.

"Your Highness what is it?", Xin spoke quietly

"If we do as you suggest it means that only I can fight Raulf, as no other will be a match for him", Jai spoke slowly. "As much as I hate him for what he has done, I don't know if I could kill my brother!".

All three went silent after Jai had spoken, all caught up in their own thoughts, the implications of what Prince Jai had just said running through their minds.

CHAPTER TEN

Storm, Rebel and Katrina were now only a few hours ride away from Druk Palace, having ridden hard with no stops along the way.

"I need to stop", Katrina said slowing down her horse and started to veer her horse towards a stream close by. The other two followed suit jumping of their horses as they neared the stream. They all unsaddled their horses to let them graze and get a drink from the stream. Rebel took some apples from his saddlebag giving one to each of the three horses, biting into one himself he made his way to the stream.

Katrina had sat down cross-legged on the grass close to the stream and closed her eyes, "Prince Jai can you hear me?" Katrina tried to connect with Jai but with no response. She tried again, and again nothing. Opening her eyes, she looked up at Storm and Rebel, "I cannot get hold of Prince Jai. I have tried a number of times but to no avail, I hope that all is well", Katrina spoke with concern in her voice.

"I am sure all will be well dear, I think we should continue on our journey back to the Kingdom soon", Storm trailed off staring at the stream with amazement on his face. Katrina turned to see what Storm was looking at and gasped.

Rebel was playing with the stream water controlling it, the water was spouting up high into the sky. Rebel was shaping it into all sorts of shapes and patterns. The fish in the stream were jumping up and down and weaving through the water with delight. Rebel was laughing out loud at what they were saying to him.

"Katrina, Storm, the fish are talking to me, it's amazing… how can I understand them?" Rebel looked quickly at both of them and then back to the stream continuing with the game he was playing.

"Rebel stop that please!", exclaimed Storm speaking firmly, "We must leave now".

Rebel looked at Storm and then Katrina, the expressions on their faces told him they were not joking. He slowly lowered the water and the fish back into the stream.

"Rebel dear, I know you are discovering the extent of your powers, but please be aware of letting anyone see you doing this. We must keep this a secret until we speak to the King", Katrina said quietly as she mounted her horse.

Rebel mounted his horse and sheepishly looked at both Storm and Katrina, "Sorry both I just couldn't help it, I could hear the fish talking to me and before I knew it, it just happened". Storm shook his head, a small grin on his face, "Come on Rebel let us go, before you get us all in trouble." Storm rode ahead quickly with the other two following close behind.

They had been riding for a couple of hours, when finally, they could see Druk Palace in the distance. Before long they were at the gates of the palace, like the Queen and Prince Jai before them, they were also refused entry. As before, the guard told them that the Queen and then Prince Jai had made their way to the Peoples Library.

Storm glared at the guard ignoring what he said and spoke commandingly, "OPEN THE GATES NOW, the King awaits us", looking then at Katrina, "Katrina please make your way to the Peoples Library and bring the Queen and Prince Jai back to the Palace post-haste". Katrina nodded and with a quick wave turned her horse and galloped towards the People's Library.

Turning his attention back to the guard who was now quaking in his boots but still had not moved,

"I commend you guard, for you are loyal to your King and have done your duty well, but we will have to enter so stand aside if you do not wish to be hurt". Storm then looked at Rebel, "Rebel lad opens the gates quickly let us go to the King".

The guard looked on in amazement as the gates just flew open. He quickly moved out of the way as Storm and Rebel rode through. "Oh, and when the Queen comes make sure you let her in", Storm shouted as he passed the frightened guard.

They rode quickly towards the palace courtyard and jumped off their horses shouting to the stable master to come and take the horses. As they approached the entrance to the palace, they could see Mercy and Beda standing guard outside.

Rebel hailed them both, Mercy saw him first and ran towards him. To his surprise, Mercy gave him a big hug holding him tightly. Realising what she had done Mercy quickly pushed him away and started talking quickly, "We were told by the King to guard the doors and allow nobody in. We're not sure what is happening, but they are all in the Contemplation Hall", Mercy finished a little flustered, her cheeks had turned rosy and her eyes were glowing brightly.

Realisation dawned on Rebel that Mercy liked him and started grinning like an idiot. Storm nudged him and pushed him towards the doors looking at Mercy then Rebel with a sly grin on his face, "Let's go Rebel plenty of time for all that once we've done what we need to", said Storm laughing at Rebel whose grin got wider at what Storm had intimated.

As they approached the main entrance of the Palace, they both hesitated and looked at each other acknowledging silently that something was seriously wrong. They approached the entrance entering cautiously, Rebel held Storm back with one hand and placed one finger on his lips indicating to Storm to be silent.

There was total and utter silence, not a sound could be heard. Usually, the Palace was a noisy place bustling with people coming and going. They made their way slowly into the main corridor of the palace, both drawing their weapons in readiness of any potential trouble.

Storm held in his hand a short sword which had appeared from nowhere, Rebel looked at Storm with surprise as he had never seen Storm with a weapon before.

Rebel held a silver dagger given to him by his father. He had always worn it, hidden on the inside of his left boot, since his father had gifted it to him when he had been sent to the Palace.

As they approached the great hall of the Palace, they noticed that everyone within were frozen in time. All looked as though they had been frozen in the middle of whatever task they were performing. Some were mid-stride, others were bending over the fire in the process of putting more logs on, although the fire itself was now stone-cold with only ashes in the hearth remaining.

Others were just sitting in small groups around the tables of the great hall, frozen in time. Some were holding drinks in their hands and others were obviously in the middle of their evening meal. The overall feeling was eerily scary.

Storm looked at Rebel indicating that they should move on. They both slowly made their way out of the room. As they continued to make their way towards the Contemplation Hall, they could see people frozen in a moment of time.

"What has happened here?", whispered Rebel.

"It looks as though Zi has managed to stop time, something I thought I would never see in my lifetime", Storm spoke quietly.

As they approached the Contemplation Hall, they could see more frozen people, some crowded around the door, some with their ears against it as if they were trying to listen to what was being said behind the closed doors. The entrance was blocked by all the bodies clustered around it.

Storm and Rebel started to physically pick some of them up and move them away from the doors, so they could gain access.

Slowly they opened the doors not quite sure what to expect on the other side. As they peered in, they could see nothing, the room was empty. They both made their way in cautiously closing the door behind them.

"What time is it Rebel lad?", Storm asked

"Well looking at the sun I would say it's coming up to dusk", Rebel said looking out of one of the huge windows in the Hall.

Storm made his way to some chairs at the side of the room where he could see tables still laden with food. The meat juices had congealed on the plates, hovering above the plates Storm could also see flies that had also frozen suspended in time, with some frozen on the food itself.

"Ughh disgusting", muttered Rebel.

"Come sit here Rebel, we shall wait", Storm instructed.

"What are we waiting for Storm?", Rebel asked as he took a seat next to him.

"You shall see shortly", with that Storm went silent closing his eyes.

They sat there for nearly two hours and Rebel could not stop fidgeting only stopping when Storm gave him a disapproving look.

Suddenly, something started to flash in the middle of the room, both Storm and Rebel jumped up from their chairs. They moved backwards slowly to stand with their backs against the wall.

The flashes started to turn into a very bright rotating light, which was going extremely fast. The heat from the light was warming their faces and Rebel could feel the sweat slowly trickling down from his forehead.

The light continued to rotate at speed for a few minutes before it started to slow down. Colours and shapes started to appear, soon it slowed to the point that they could see the figures of people as well as moans and groans coming from within the circle.

Rebel could make out the familiar faces of King Varick and Master Zi and when it eventually stopped rotating, Rebel moved towards the two.

Some of the High Elders started to fall backwards with others starting to vomit uncontrollably.

Zi stood up quickly making his way towards the King, who was by now lying on his back looking sickly. Storm and Rebel had started to help some of the others to chairs sitting them down and getting them some water.

"Highness, please allow me to help you", as he spoke Zi touched King Varick on the shoulder, Varick immediately felt better and struggled to sit up.

Patting Varick on the shoulder, Zi made his way around the room doing the same for the others.

A little unsteady on his feet Varick managed to stand up when he noticed Storm and Rebel. He gestured to them to come close.

"It's good to see you lad, you too Storm, please fill me in on what has happened over the past three days", Varick stood up and made his way to some chairs. Sitting down he indicated to them both to do the same.

Zi made his way across having helped the others. As he did so, he reverted back to his normal height and sat down next to Varick, "Yes, Storm please continue", Zi said smiling at him.

Storm was nearing the end of his report when Queen Althea, Prince Jai, Katrina, Crick and Librarian Xin came rushing into the room. As soon as they saw the King, they quickly made their way across to him.

Behind them some of the serving staff also came in looking a little dazed. They made their way quickly to the tables, as they approached, they could see the state of the food and started to look scared, turning towards the Queen bowing low as they were unsure of what had happened.

Varick noticed what was happening and instructed them to rise and clear the tables and to bring fresh food and wine quickly. He also instructed them to ensure that the rest of the Palace was checked and cleaned too.

With that he turned his attention back to the others.

Crick made his way to his brother Dribble, embracing him in a bear hug. Varick had jumped to his feet and clasped Queen Althea to his chest with one arm and hugged his son Jai in the other.

After a few minutes, Zi interrupted and asked them all to gather around the tables that the servants had just set with chairs. Zi also ushered the High Elders to sit as well.

"My King, if I may, we must now plan quickly to stop Prince Raulf getting hold of the Colors of Flamecore and organise everyone to get ready for the Games which are due to take place in two weeks' time. During the Thunder moon" ... Zi spoke firmly but softly, and all listened because now they all knew who he was, except those who had just arrived.

Prince Jai interrupted, ... "I'm not sure Master Zi that you are the right person to organise this...", when Jai was intervened by Shahmaran who had now changed back to her human form, Manasa, High Elder of the Serpentes.

Your Highness Prince Jai, unknown to you, Master Zi is Tai Sui the God of Age, and as such he is exactly the right person to instruct us" ... as she spoke, she bowed her head in deference to Zi.

Prince Jai looked shocked and turned to his father for confirmation, Varick nodded and then indicated to Zi to continue. Prince Jai looked on in absolute amazement at what he had just learnt.

"Master Zi, if I may?", spoke Prince Jai, with nothing but awe and respect in his voice and demeanour towards Zi, now that he knew who he was... "We have discovered a possible solution to the games and how we could stop Raulf from getting a Key to the Heavenly Gates".

"Yes! Master Zi", Librarian Xin was positioned just behind the chair on which Rebel was sitting. "King Varick needs to change the Shengxiao Games to the original Dragon Games as they were played many years ago. In this way only the Dragonian Clan can take part and all the other keys remain with the current eleven families. The twelfth key will then remain with the Dragonian family, however depending on which family of the Dragon Clans wins, will determine who will be King!

By doing this the Ratticus Family can appoint their High Elder and keep their Key", Librarian Xin finished speaking and looked on in silence at the King as Varick absorbed the information given to him.

The room erupted with everyone talking all at once at what Xin had relayed to them. When Prince Jai suddenly stood up and silenced them all with a loud command and a wave of his hands.

"What Librarian Xin did not tell you, was that the Dragon Games are to the death and the only one who can challenge my brother Prince Raulf is me, as I am the only other Prince of the Dragonian Clan, and I do not think I could kill my brother". Jai had spoken softly, his voice petering off as he finished speaking.

Everyone in the room had gone silent as they looked at Prince Jai and then the King. Queen Althea had collapsed to the ground by King Varick's feet as she absorbed what Prince Jai had said and was weeping quietly at the thought of what may lay ahead for her two sons.

Varick held his wife's hands and looked at Zi, "Is this the only way Zi?", Varick asked quietly.

Zi looked at Varick and then transferred his gaze to Rebel. Varick followed his gaze and then looked back at him wide-eyed, NO, not Rebel, not any of them, IS THERE NOT ANOTHER WAY?"

"Your Majesty", this time Katrina replied, "Rebel is ready he can do this!"

"I don't understand how Rebel can take part in the games he is not a Prince!", exclaimed Prince Jai who had jumped up from his chair with indignation.

"Sit down Jai", commanded Varick, then sighing he spoke again, "Unbeknown to all of you Rebel is a Prince, and he is your cousin Jai. His father is my brother Prince Tarrin".

Shocked the room went silent as all took in the enormity of what Varick had revealed to them.

"Why did you not tell us this before? Why have you been hiding this from us?". This came from one of the High Elders who looked at Varick accusingly and gave Rebel a look of animosity.

Rebel was not surprised at the animosity emanating from the High Elders, as part of his role as the Kings advisor he had been undercover and had infiltrated many of the families. Now they all looked warily at him as they realised that he knew far more than they would have told him had they known he was a Prince.

"Before you all start having a go at Rebel, he did not know his heritage. I kept it from him for good reason", Varick spoke with authority that dared anyone to challenge him.

He is innocent in this deception. Let us focus on the issue at hand, the games and Prince Raulf", Varick looked at Zi as he spoke.

"Your Majesty Prince Raulf is currently caught in a time loop within the Forbidden Steps with Princess Sofia. I managed to speak to the Princess and instructed her on how to trap Prince Raulf. This was imperative as he was opening too many Chaos Portals, and this would have been catastrophic for the Kingdom.

I believe that they will be released from the time loop shortly if Princess Sofia has done exactly what I instructed", Zi finished speaking and looked at Katrina.

"Kat, please can you see if you can reach Sofia and ascertain the current situation?", Zi smiled as he spoke to Katrina and then looked at Varick.

"Your Majesty, I suggest we all convene to the antechamber and await news on Raulf and Sofia. It may take Katrina a short while to reach Sofia". Zi then made his way across the hall with the others following suit.

Varick instructed all the High Elders to go and freshen up and meet back in the Hall in an hour. He entered the antechamber and closed the door behind him.

"Sophia? Sophia can you hear me?", Katrina had been trying to contact Sophia for nearly thirty minutes to no avail. Suddenly, a faint thought entered her head. Katrina focused on the faint words which had entered her mind.

"Katrina, Katrina I can hear you. Are you still there?", ever so faintly, then a little louder, "Katrina?

“Yes, yes my child I am here. How are you?”

“Thank goodness I thought I would never get through to you. I am still within the Forbidden Steps time-loop and we have only fifteen more time-loops to go, is it okay to finish now and get out of this nightmare?”,…

“I will ask Zi now and get back to you straight away Sophia. Be patient it will not be long now before all this will be over, I hope!” Katrina quickly relayed this to Sophia as she hurriedly made her way to the antechamber where the group had gathered.

All in the room looked up at Katrina as she burst into the room.

“Master Zi, I have contacted Sophia, she has fifteen more time-loops to go, she asks if it is okay to finish now, or should she continue?”

Zi pondered for a few minutes before replying, “Assuming each loop takes ten minutes ask her to do a further ten more loops to give us time to discuss the games and their format. In the meantime”, Zi turned towards Rebel and Storm, …

“You two must go to the Forbidden Steps and take a contingent of Royal Guards with you to escort Prince Raulf back to the Palace.

Whatever you do, DO NOT ENGAGE HIM IN ANY WAY, we do not want anything to happen until the games are announced formally and more importantly, we do not know how powerful he has become since being down there”.

“Perhaps, Master Zi, I should go and meet Raulf”, spoke King Varick.

"He cannot confront me or hurt me directly as I am King and as such protected from magical powers that may be used against me!".

"You are right your Majesty, please be careful and perhaps Katrina can go with you as she also has very powerful magic". Zi glanced towards Katrina as he spoke and also noted the expression on Storm's face when Katrina was mentioned.

"Storm you do not need to worry yourself, I know of Katrina's capabilities, she will be more than capable of dealing with Raulf. Your Majesty before you leave, let us discuss the decision for the Games". Zi sat down and motioned for the others to do the same.

Queen Althea, Prince Jai, Katrina, Crick, Librarian Xin, Dribble, and Rebel all sat down at an extremely long table which was situated in the centre of the antechamber. The table was also carved from a single redwood, the top of the table was polished to such a sheen that you could see your face in it, it was magnificent. It could easily seat twenty people, although only twelve chairs had been placed around it.

King Varick and Master Zi sat at one end of the table and the others looked at them both expectantly.

King Varick looked at Librarian Xin, "Librarian Xin, what can you tell us about the Dragon Games?", Varick asked quietly.

"Your Majesty, the origins of the games are older than the Games of Shengxiao, which were introduced by the Gods two hundred years ago. The Dragon Games took place every year in the seventh month, the month of the Thunder Moon.

The main difference between the two Games, is that the Dragon Games only involved the Dragonian Clan. They were held to determine who the next King would be, and thereby the next ruling dragon family. As the ruling family they were the only ones who had access to the Heavenly Gates. These games were fought to the death, which resulted in many of the Dragonian Clan losing their strongest warriors due to the nature of the prize.

The Shengxiao games were introduced by the Gods for a number of reasons. Firstly, to protect the lineage of the Dragonian Clan, and secondly to allow access to the Heavenly Gates to more of the Kingdom's Families. The Shengxiao Games have allowed the Kingdom to flourish and prosper and have served the Gods well". Librarian Xin finished speaking and bowed low to both King Varick and Master Zi.

All in the room were silent as Librarian Xin finished speaking. King Varick was also silent as he pondered on what he had heard. After a long silence Varick finally spoke to the group.

"I feel we have no choice in the matter if we are to maintain some semblance of normality in the Kingdom, the games must be played in their original form. So, this year the Dragon Games will start on the night of the Thunder Moon. This way we will be following the rules set originally by the games", Varick looked at Master Zi as he finished speaking, who in turn nodded his head in agreement of the decision.

“Rebel lad and Storm, you two will represent the Dragonian Clan. Librarian Xin, you will be in charge of the games and their organisation. It is imperative that they are played exactly to the rules of the original games. This is the only way the people and the Gods will accept the change to the games. But, please note that this is a one-time only change to the games, next year the original Shengxiao Games will resume. Master Zi I am assuming that this is acceptable to the Gods?” finished Varick.

“Yes, I will confer with them Varick, but I see no issue. Librarian Xin I believe you are fully aware of the rules for the original games already?”, asked Zi.

“Indeed, I am Master Zi”, nodded Xin.

CHAPTER ELEVEN

Sophia was getting really tired and was starting to flag. It was becoming more and more difficult to maintain the time-loop. Only four more to go, and she had to finish as instructed by Katrina. Raulf was decidedly livid and held Sophia's wrist tightly as he was afraid of being left behind in the time-loop by Sophia.

"Sophia, it's Katrina, can you hear me?", Katrina's voice filtered through to Sophia's thoughts. "Yes, yes I can Katrina", Katrina could sense that Sophia was struggling.

"We are here Sophia, just by the entrance to the Forbidden Steps. Do your last time-loop and then say the correct sequence of words to get out. I have been told by Master Zi that once you say the correct sequence you will find yourself back at the top of the stairs by the entrance. As soon as you arrive there try to move away from Raulf as quickly as you can. Do you understand me Sophia?', Katrina had spoken quickly and was hoping that Sophia had heard all the instructions she had given.

"Yes, I heard all you said Katrina, I will be ready!". Katrina then broke the link.

Sophia found herself at the top of the stairs when she started the sequence of words....

"Forbidden Flamecore Lets All Men Enter Steps"
As she spoke the last word, Sophia had a feeling of moving through air very quickly, finding herself with Raulf at the top of the stairs by the entrance of the Forbidden Steps.

Sophia was disorientated, but she clearly remembered Katrina's' instructions. She twisted her arm free from Raulf moving quickly away. At the same time, she saw her father move towards Raulf and throw a cloak over him. As he did so Varick muttered the words, "HOLD FAST".

Raulf found himself bound tight by the cloak. No matter what he did he could not move. As he struggled, he felt himself falling landing on the floor with a thump. The cloak had wrapped itself around the full length of him and held him tightly. Raulf struggled unable to loosen the hold of the cloak. It was the Caysand cloak, Raulf recognised it and knowing he was trapped he stopped struggling and just lay there fuming.

Varick rushed to Sophia, "My darling Sophia are you okay dear?".

"Father, father I am so happy to see you. Are mother and Jai safe? I have not seen either since Raulf took me away from mother", Sophia sobbed as she held on tightly to her father the King.

"Your Majesty we should make haste and leave the Nest quickly, as per High Elder Manasa instructed. We cannot let the Serpentes know we are within the Nest as It will cause too much trouble for all involved", Katrina spoke urgently and started to usher the King and Princess Sophia back up the tunnel.

"Guards bind Prince Raulf's mouth quickly as we cannot allow him to alert anyone. Quickly, quickly", Katrina instructed.

The guards did just that and one of the Kings Guard who was extremely tall and strong hoisted Raulf over his shoulder and moved hastily behind the disappearing group in front of him.

Sophia held on to her father as Katrina led the group back through the tunnels to the entrance where High Elder Manasa was waiting. They all made their way outside quickly and quietly, once the last person was out Manasa sealed the entrance then followed the group as they all made their way down the hill to where the horses had been tethered.

The guard who was holding Raulf carefully put him across his horse and mounted up behind him. Princess Sophia was riding behind her father holding on tightly. Once all were mounted, they started single file towards the main road which led to the palace.

Before long they were all galloping toward the Palace leaving the Serpentes Nest behind them. The closer they got to the palace, Varick could feel Sophia loosen her hold on him and start to relax a little. Varick had a determined look on his face as his thoughts wandered to the next problem, the Games. He would do anything in his power to ensure that Rebel survived the Games.

Varick's brother Prince Tarrin would not forgive him if anything happened to Rebel. He would not forgive himself if any happened to Rebel; he had come to love him like his own son, and he was angry at Raulf for putting him and the Kingdom in such a position.

Tarrin had just finished in the stables and was making his way to the house to wash up for the evening, when he saw dust rising in the distance. He was surprised at this as he had very few visitors and those who did come, he normally expected. This was unusual and his interest piqued.

It was too far for him to make out who it was so Tarrin transformed into his dragon and leapt into the sky. As Tarrin was winging his way towards the visitor, he looked down to earth and far below on the ground he could see a small black panther running fast in the same direction he was going.

Tarrin smiled as he recognised his wife Lexi in her animal form. She was always one step ahead of him, as her Panthera heritage and being royalty too, gave her abilities that were unique to the Panthera Family Royals.

Both Tarrin and Lexi were a very private couple, neither of them liked unknowns to come close to their home. They would rather stop this person in their tracks before they got too close.

Tarrin had flown ahead of Lexi and was nosediving towards the intruder. As he got closer, he recognised the male rider and slowed his descent. The rider stopped as he didn't want to spook his horse too much at the sight of Tarrin in his dragon form.

Just as Tarrin landed Lexi arrived, both had transformed back to their human forms.

Tarrin was surprised to see that it was Conall, the Master

of the Royal Guard. It had been many years since he had seen him last and the years had been kind to him. Conall had trained both Varick and himself in sword skills and dragon flight.

As Tarrin walked towards him, he realised that he had missed him and his old life. Nostalgia overwhelmed him as he welcomed Conall.

Tarrin clasped Conall's hands in his, and then gave him a big bear hug.

"Conall man, what brings your old bones to this part of the world and why did you not fly? It has been an age. Is all well?", Tarrin asked gruffly.

"Sadly, Your Majesty, all is not well, I come to bring you back to the Kingdom". Conall breathed out heavily and looked weary as the ride had been long and arduous, having taken him three long days to get to the homeland of the Panthera's known as The Range. "Also, I am unable to fly, but that is not important at the moment I will fill you in at a later date as the reason why", Conall spoke with regret in his voice.

"Come Conall, let us go back to the house where you can freshen up and take some food. You can fill us in properly then on what transpires within the Kingdom", Lexi spoke firmly but with a warmth in her voice which encouraged them all to move in the direction of the homestead.

They had all decided to walk back as the weather was warm and the evening breeze had just started to blow gently cooling them down as they made their way back. The sun was just disappearing behind the mountains in the horizon to the North, when they finally arrived at the homestead.

Lexi started preparing the evening meal and was setting it on the table when Conall and Tarrin came back into the living area after a wash and a change of clothes.

"Please sit Conall and eat, don't let the meal go cold", Lexi indicating to a chair close to the fire as she spoke. They all sat down and ate the meal quietly and quickly. When they had finished Lexi quickly cleared the table, bringing some ale for all of them and setting it down on the table. "Please Conall, tell us what is happening in the Kingdom that I am required to go back", Tarrin encouraged.

Conall started to explain in detail what had transpired in the Kingdom, leaving nothing out. They had finished two cups of ale by the time he had finished speaking. Silence filled the room, Conall looked at Tarrin, then at Lexi and he could see thoughts that were flitting through their minds mirrored on their faces. The overwhelming expression on both faces was of concern and worry about their son, Rebel.

Conall broke the silence, "I think Sire you should know that all in the Kingdom are now aware that Rebel is your son and nephew to the King. It is for this very reason that we can perhaps beat Raulf at his own game.

Rebel is more powerful than any of us could have known, which is why Master Zi has chosen him to compete in the Games", Conall finished looking directly at Tarrin with a sad smile on his face.

Tarrin stood up quickly, his chair falling back behind him. "Lexi, please prepare for us to leave in the morning. Rebel needs us, as does Varick and the Kingdom", turning to Conall, Tarrin gave a grateful look.

"Thank you Conall for coming, rest this night as tomorrow at dawn we leave for Shengxiao", looking at Lexi, Tarrin spoke softly. "Lexi dear, I will be outside for a short while and will come to bed soon".

With that Tarrin went outside and made his way to the stables. Lexi knew where he had gone. Tarrin had gone to get that which he had buried a long time ago when he was asked to leave the Kingdom of Shengxiao for marrying her.

Lexi looked sadly at Conall, "Come Conall, let me show you where you can rest for the night", leading him to a small bed chamber at the back of the house. She bade him good night and made her way slowly to her own bed chamber.

Tarrin entered the stables and made his way past the stalls where the horses were kept towards a small room at the far-left hand corner of the building.

The room was padlocked, Tarrin took out a large bronze key which was attached to a leather thong around his neck. The lock was rusty with age and Tarrin had to jiggle it a bit before the key finally turned and the lock snapped open.

Tarrin hesitated for a moment, then taking a deep breath he entered the room. It was a very small room with no windows and barely five by five feet in size.

In one corner of the room was a huge wooden chest with the crest of a dragon carved into the top laid with gold and a gold circlet was embossed just above the head of the dragon. As a prince of the realm, Tarrin had access to many riches, all of which he had left behind when he left Shengxiao. What was in the box was all he had brought with him of his past life.

Tarrin opened the box slowly and a plume of dust accompanied by a musty smell assailed his nostrils. Turning his head to one side he sneezed loudly before fully lifting the lid back and letting it rest against the wall behind it.

Folded neatly on top was a cloak of Caysand, one of a matching pair made by his father and gifted to Varick and Tarrin on their respective Eighteenth Birthyear. It was an extremely precious gift and one that Tarrin could not leave behind when he left the Kingdom. He lifted it out slowly. It still looked as new as it did on the day it was given to him, such was the power of Caysand, and placed it on the floor next to him.

Next, he pulled out two wrist cuffs made of silver which were carved with the crest of the Dragonian Clan. These were his war cuffs, and they let everyone know that he was not only Prince of the realm but also General of the Shengxiao Army. It had hurt him to the core to leave his soldiers, but it had to be done.

Finally, the last item in the box was his Crown as Prince of Shengxiao. The crown like the cloak was made of Caysand and it glistened even in the dark little room. Embedded in the circlet was a dazzling blue sapphire which signified his rank as a Prince of the Realm.

Right at the bottom of the box was a plain black leather bag. He pulled it out and put the items into the bag after which he closed the wooden box. Hefting the bag over his shoulder Tarrin made his way back to the house. This time he did not bother to lock the small room in the stable leaving it wide open.

Tarrin put the black leather bag at the foot of the bed and crawled under the covers next to Lexi. Tarrin had many thoughts running through his head as he held Lexi from behind. It took a long time for him to finally get to sleep.

CHAPTER TWELVE

Prince Jai entered the Contemplation Hall having freshened up with a bath and a fresh change of clothes. Many of the High Elders had already gathered, but he noticed that a few were still missing.

The aroma of fresh hot food and drink which had been laid out on the tables along one side of the room beckoned him. He noticed the servants were waiting for instructions to serve, and he nodded to them to continue.

Prince Jai turned to the gathered group, "Distinguished High Elders please partake in some refreshments whilst we wait for the others to arrive. Once everyone is here, I will explain all", Raulf finished determined not to get caught up with answering questions that he could see some of the High Elders were itching to ask.

Instead, he quickly made his way to the tables laden with food and piled a plate high from the various dishes in front of him. Jai was famished having not eaten properly since his capture. He grabbed a tankard of ale and sat down at a table on one side of the room. As some came to sit with him, he discouraged them with a look. He needed time to think and prepare what he needed to say. It was imperative he got it right as his father had stressed to him.

A short while later when everyone had finished eating,

Prince Jai stood up and made his way to a point in the room where he could face them all. The High Elders had sat down in anticipation of what Prince Jai was going to announce, all going silent when they saw him come to the front. Prince Jai stood still and looked at them all before he started to speak.

"I am not sure if you are all aware of what has transpired over the last ten days, so I will start at the beginning".

Prince Jai started to relay exactly what had happened from the challenge made by Jonas, to the kidnapping of his mother, sister and himself by Raulf. The role Raulf had played in Jonas making the challenge and how the Serpentes Nest had been involved. The main concern here Prince Jai explained was that unknowingly Raulf had now made a challenge that could potentially affect any one of the twelve families as they would all potentially have to play the games to keep their family Keys.

Murmuring and outcry within the High Elders disrupted what Jai was going to say next. Jai held up his hands and silenced the group. "Please listen, your King, my father has found a solution that will not affect any of you". Everyone in the room sat down, going silent in eager anticipation of what was going to be said next.

Continuing Jai talked about how Raulf had started to open the Chaos Portals, at the mention of the Chaos Portals some in the room exclaimed their horror and distress at hearing this. Jai recognised the High Elders in question.

They were the High Elders of the Oxbow Herd, Adira and Janesh and High Elders of the Canis Pack, Briana and Duke. He had a feeling that they may have been the ones who were aware of the Chaos Portals as they went a long way back having been High Elders for many years.

Carrying on Jai went on to explain who Master Zi was and as Tai Sui the God of Age he was able to stop time. He knew that the High Elders in the room were aware of this as they had been asked to take part in this act by King Varick with Zi in his true form as Tai Sui guiding them.

Jai moved quickly on to Raulf being trapped within the Forbidden Steps by his sister Sophia, as he attempted to get hold of the "Flamecore". Sophia had managed to trap him within the steps, Jai explained, so that Zi could stop Raulf opening more of the Chaos Portals, as this would have put the whole Kingdom of Shengxiao into danger.

The High Elders were becoming agitated and angry at what they were hearing. Questions were now starting to be asked that Jai was not ready to answer yet.

"Please, please, a little more patience I am coming to the end and will explain to you how we will deal with the situation," Jai placated them.

Prince Jai hesitated, before taking a deep breath, "What you did not know and neither did I until a few hours ago is that Rebel is the son of Prince Tarrin, nephew to the King and my cousin".

As Jai had expected the room erupted with noise and questions at this revelation. The High Elders shouting at Prince Jai about being tricked by the King and some even suggesting that plots against the Twelve Families in the Kingdom may have been instigated by Rebel and the King himself.

Jai silenced them with a huge roar as the dragon in him came out in anger at the allegations being thrown at this father. The room abruptly fell silent will all sitting back down looking a little cowed. They had not seen Jai angry before and all were intimidated by him.

Jai again took another deep breath, although this time it was to contain his dragon self and calmed his voice before he continued to speak.

"To conclude, it has been decided that the games this year will be played in the month of the Thunder Moon. They will be played in their original form as the "Dragon Games".

This means that all your Keys are safe. Only the Key to the Dragonian Clan will be available in the challenge. The competition as decreed by his Highness King Varick will be against Prince Raulf with his partner Jonas of the Glaring and Prince Rebel and his partner Storm of the Felinia Black". Jai went silent to let this information be absorbed by the gathering.

Jai noticed that Janesh High Elder of the Oxbow Herd had stood up and then amazingly he started to clap, slowly at first and then with vigour. Following close behind him High Elder Duke from the Canis Pack followed suit. Before long everyone in the room had stood up and were cheering.

Jai bemused at what he was witnessing took a few minutes before he waved them down to sit. However, Janesh stayed standing,

"Your highness, words cannot express my pride at being

a High Elder at this time of extreme danger to the Kingdom. The way your father King Varick has resolved the situation is more than satisfactory to the Oxbow Herd. In fact, we are humbled that he has put the lives of his family in this situation so that the Kingdom remains safe.

We remain loyal to the Dragonians your Highness, and will aid them in any way we can", with that Janesh made his way to where Prince Jai was standing and went on one knee and kissed his hand to demonstrate his fealty.

A queue had formed behind him and one by one High Elders of each of the Eleven Families followed suit.

Jai thanked them all, then announced that they should all make their way outside to the field where the Master Zi and Rebel were waiting for them.

As they all made their way out into the courtyard, Varick was riding in with his group after rescuing Sophia and capturing Raulf. Jai could clearly see Sophia riding behind their father. Jai whooped with joy at seeing them both and ran towards them as they slowed to a halt near the main entrance of the palace. The stable hands came running towards them to take care of the horses.

Jai helped Sophia off his father's mount and hugged her close, "Thank the gods that you are okay", Jai whispered into her ear. As he looked over her shoulder, he could see a royal guard with something held in front of him. Not sure what it was he started towards the guard in curiosity.

"No, Jai do not go there, it is Raulf, I have wrapped him in the Caysand Cloak, he is unable to speak or move. I suggest you stay away from him until we are ready to release him". Varick spoke with authority and Jai glanced up at him and then looked at Raulf. Shaking his head Jai turned back round to help his sister into the palace.

Varick instructed the guard to take Raulf to his bedroom and to stand guard outside his door. "Take another guard with you", Varick shouted at him as he strode away to follow Jai and Sophia into the Palace.

"Your Majesty", Katrina spoke quickly before Varick disappeared through the doors, Queen Shahmaran and I will make our way to the gaming fields to assist Storm and Master Zi?"

"Sorry Katrina, yes you are right, I was so caught up with getting Sophia back, I forgot about that. Let us go together", Varick replied and turned back towards Katrina and Shahmaran.

They made their way quickly through the grounds of the palace to the gaming fields, where in the distance they could see the group gathered to one side of the huge field. As they approached the group, they could hear Librarian Xin speaking.

Xin speaking. "The Thunder Dragons must be involved Highness", he said insistently to Rebel.

"Stop calling me Highness Xin, just call be Rebel please",Rebel looked uncomfortable as Librarian Xin insisted on calling him Highness.

"Rebel lad, Librarian Xin is correct in addressing you as Highness, get used to it!". Varick spoke with a firmness which brooked no argument.

"What were you saying about the Thunder Dragons, Xin. Why do they have to be involved in this?", Varick addressed Xin questioningly.

"Sire, they are part of the Dragonian Clan and when the games were originally played as the Dragon games, they formed a key part of the games, so they must be involved". Xin looked at both Varick and Rebel as he spoke.

"You do realise Xin that the Thunder Dragons have tried for years to get hold of the Crown and have tried many things to achieve this. If we allow them to take part in the games, it will make it even more dangerous for Rebel and Storm. As the Thunder Dragons do not fight fair", Varick spoke hoping to change the fact, but realising that there would be no choice in the matter.

If the Dragon Games were to be played then they had to be played to the rules, and that included all the Dragon Clans.

"Err You Highness, one other thing I must raise that you will not like I think", Xin spoke with hesitation.

"What is it Xin? Speak up man". Varick looked at him with impatience.

"Well your Majesty, as per the rules of the Dragon Games, the part of the games which involves the Element Water must be played in the City of Adraga, home of the Thunder Dragons. This is to make it fair for all the Clans", Xin finished speaking and went silent.

All in the group stood silently as they absorbed this information. It was Queen Shahmaran, who spoke first.

"So be it, if thisss isss what must be done, we have no choice in the matter. Let us prepare Rebel and Storm for the challenges ahead and not waste any more time. Librarian Xin is there anything else you need to tell us, or is that it?"

"There are no more rules Queen Shahmaran, however, we are all aware that the Dragon Games are played to the death. We are hopeful that Prince Rebel and Storm will be successful in this endeavour I can do some research on the games involving the Element Water to see if we can gain some insight and thereby advantage". Xin looked towards Varick for instructions.

"Thank you Librarian Xin, yes please find out what is involved in the Water Games and get back to us as soon as possible", Varick nodded his agreement then turned to the rest of the group as Xin left to go back to the People's Library.

Turning to Master Zi, "Zi my friend, I would ask you to go to the home of the Thunder Dragons as my emissary and inform them of the games. They will need time to prepare for the Water Element games to take place in Adraga.

Please keep us informed of what is happening. Thank you, my friend." Varick clasped Zi's hand and forearm in a gesture of the close relationship they had.

"Your Highness I will leave immediately and shall communicate with Katrina via mind meld to keep you informed". Zi looked at Katrina for agreement. Katrina nodded and held

Storm's hand.

Storm put his arm around Katrina, knowing what she was thinking. The challenge to the death was playing on his mind too. He wasn't concerned about himself. He was more worried about Rebel wondering if in fact he was ready for this. Storm knew the Thunder Dragons were cunning, they would fight to death no matter what.

CHAPTER THIRTEEN

The city of Adraga was home to the Thunder Dragons. Adraga's coastline stretched as far as the eye could see in both directions. The coastline was nearly one hundred leagues long and the full length of it was covered in Caysand.

Caysand had magical properties, which if used properly, could take on a number of magical elements. So precious was it that it was decreed by the Gods that only the rulers of the Kingdom of Shengxiao could use it, as long they ensured that it was kept safe from all others. When a distant forefather of King Varick had become King, it had remained under the rule of the Ledary Dragons. Until now, that rule was never in question.

The main purpose in life for the Thunder Dragons was to guard the Caysand. This duty had been given to them by the very first King of Shengxiao and all others who followed kept the tradition as the Thunder Dragons had done an excellent job of keeping the Caysand safe.

The leader of the Thunder Dragons, Zale had tried many times, to challenge Varick, but to no avail. The Gods had decreed that the twelve keys were the only way to have access into the Kingdom of Shengxiao and the Key for the Draconians was held by Varick as King of the Clan.

Zale had already been informed through the grapevine

that a Key had become available, which had belonged to the Ratticus Family. To this end Zale had already started to make plans to attend the games which were due to take place in the month of the Thunder Moon.

Zale had been delighted when he had heard this. It was excellent news as the Thunder Moon was particularly auspicious for the Thunder Dragons. Added to that, during the time the moon was in its full phase, the Thunder Dragons were at their most powerful.

Their power became stronger as the Thunder Dragons had the ability to absorb the energy from the lightening in the sky. When a storm was due the Thunder Dragons took to the sky waiting for the lightening and flying directly into a strike to absorb the energy.

When this happened, no enemy would mount an attack in the month of the Thunder Moon against the Thunder Dragons.

Zi entered Adraga on the eve of the sixth night. He had decided to come alone as he required no one to protect him. As yet, those in Adraga were not aware of his true form. As far as they were concerned, he was the leader of the Felinia Clowder, nothing more.

Zi was aware that the city of Adraga was not a city like any other and nothing like the Kingdom. It was in fact made up of caves which were cut into the cliffs just above the Caysand beach. The cliffs stretched at least three hundred feet high, and they continued the full length of the coastline and out of sight.

Zi had only been here once before a very long time ago before the Thunder Dragons had been asked to guard the Caysand. He could see soldiers dotted along the coast, distinct in their bronze armour which glistened in the setting sun.

As he approached the first soldier, Zi was stopped. "Who are you old man and what are you doing here?" The soldier, Zi noticed was a young man in age by dragon were known for being slow witted.

"Young man, I am Zi, Master Zi of the Felinia Clowder. I come to deliver a message to your leader Zale. The message is from King Varick of the Kingdom of Shengxiao". Zi spoke with authority hoping to impress the young soldier who did in fact look at little dim.

Before the soldier could answer, a swift flap of wings heralded the appearance of a mighty Thunder Dragon. With only two legs instead of the four like King Varick, who was ancestor to the Ledary Dragons.

The Thunder Dragons traditionally also had an extremely long tail which forked off flat and horizontally like a fish tail. This helped them move through the water with ease and it was this unique feature that could be the distinct advantage to the Thunder Dragons when the Water Element games took place.

It was Zale. Zi looked at him in admiration as Zale was a magnificent dragon, he was completely bronze in colour except for the tip of his tail and ears, which glistened gold. Zale's green eyes were also bronze flecked, as he transformed back to human. Only his eyes remained the same colour.

"Master Zi, what brings you here?", Zale's voice sounded

like a rumble of thunder in the distance.

Zale towered above Zi standing a good three feet taller than him, Zi tilted his head back to look him in the eyes.

"Greetings Zale, is there somewhere we can go and talk in private? I could do with freshening up and some refreshments before we talk", Zi finished with a smile on his face.

Zale nodded his head indicating to Zi to follow him. Dotted along the cliffs were the many caves of the Thunder Dragons. Many had small fires lit to one side of the entrance to guide those flying in.

As they made their way towards the cliffs, Zi could see a huge cave half-way up which had two huge fires lit either side of the cave. The entrance was easily fifty feet high and a hundred wide.

"Master Zi, if you please, I would ask you climb onto my back so that I can take you to my home", Zale indicated to the huge cave that Zi had spotted.

"Of course, thank you Zale". Zale transformed into his dragon and helped Zi onto his back.

"Hold tight Master Zi", Zale leapt into the air and with three strong flaps of his wings he had landed on the edge of the entrance to the cave.

Zi dismounted with the help of Zale and made his way towards a young female who was waiting a short-distance away.

"Hello", she said timidly, "my name is Ara, it means rain",

she finished with a smile.

“Master Zi, this is my daughter Ara. She always seems to know when I am home”, Zale spoke with a fond smile to Ara.

“Ara, why don’t you show Master Zi where to go, I will follow shortly”, patting Ara’s head as he spoke.

“Yes father”, Ara took Zi’s hand and led him further back into the cave. The cave was huge, within the walls of the cave the elements of Caysand sparkled like millions of stars lighting the way as they went. Eventually, Ara stopped at an antechamber the entrance of which was covered by a length of silk cloth the colour of the sea. Pulling it aside, Zi entered and was immediately struck by the beauty of the room.

One side of the room had windows carved out of the stone which allowed in the daylight. The last rays of the setting sun filtered through casting a golden glow to all corners of the room.

A huge low table was set in the middle of the room surrounded by multi-coloured cushions. Around the edges of the room a multitude of scented candles had been placed in strategic places. The scent of sandalwood and bergamot hung in the air, Zi breathed in deeply, a scent he had always loved he thought to himself.

“Please sit over here”, Ara spoke quietly in her childish voice, a smile on her face. As Zi sat down and thanked her, Zale walked in followed by some servants carrying trays of refreshments.

“Master Zi, do you wish to freshen up first before you partake in the refreshments?" Zale looked questioningly at Zi.

"No, no, I feel we must talk first Zale as time is of the essence". At the same time Zi poured himself a drink and turned towards Zale who had sat down on the opposite side of the table. Young Ara had also sat down on top of her father's lap and held her father's hand.

"As you wish Master Zi", Zale accepted the drink Zi had poured for him.

"I am sure you are aware of what transpired at the Shengxiao Games a few weeks ago Zale", started Zi.

Zale nodded and stayed silent.

"Then you also know that a Key has now become the main prize of the games. This would normally mean that all the Twelve Keys would be fought for in the games. However, as Prince Raulf created the situation, King Varick had no choice but to change the nature of the games back to the original ones played hundreds of years ago.

This year, during the month of the Thunder Moon the first Dragon Games in five hundred years will be played. By doing this the only Key at stake is the Dragonian Key. All other Keys remain with the existing families. It also means that the Thunder Dragons can now also take part in the Games to fight for the Key". Zi stopped for a moment taking a huge gulp of his drink before continuing.

"We are in the process of making the arrangements for the Games to take place at the Gaming Fields of the Palace. I come here to let you know that the Water Element Games will be played here in Adraga. They will also be the first Element Games to be played". Zi looked directly into Zales eyes as he said this, and he could see a small flicker of surprise flit across Zale's face.

"Master Zi, might I ask why you are the one who has been asked to come and relay the information to me and not one of the Royal Family? How do I know that what you are saying is true, after all you do not belong to one of the Twelve Families, you are in fact only of the Felinia Clowder". Zale who had remained polite until now, placed Ara onto a cushion next to his, and stood up. He towered above Zi hoping to intimidate him as was the usual way with the Thunder Dragons.

Zi looked up at him and shook his head slightly and stood up. As he did, he locked eyes with Zale who towered above him. Zi could see Zale's eyes getting rounder and rounder at what he was witnessing. Zale took a step back as he watched Zi start to grow in height and stature until he nearly reached the ceiling of the cave.

"What the… what tricks are these Master Zi?", Zale blustered.

"No tricks Zale, you see me now in my true form, Tai Sui the God of Age. It is I who have agreed to the Dragon Games taking place.

I come to warn you Zale, I know of the Thunder Dragons and their tricks. Take note that these Games will be played fair, otherwise you will have me to answer to. Do you understand Zale?". Zi had literally boomed this out as his voice reverberated around the caves.

Zi noticed Ara had covered her ears with her hands, and he smiled down at her to reassure her. He turned his gaze to Zale and held it until Zale looked down meekly.

Some of the guards in the bronze armour came running into the room as Zi's voice had carried far out onto the Caysand beach.

They came to a sudden halt as the first lot of soldiers saw Zi stopped in their tracks, with the others crashing in behind them. They looked at Zale for instructions.

"Leave us", commanded Zale.

"My apologies Tai Sui, I am humbled in your presence", Zale bowed low, instructing Ara to do the same.

Zi knew that Zale had slighted him by calling him by his name. However, it was not the time to punish him for this, his time would come.

"You will consult the tomes of the Thunder Dragons to plan for the Water Element Games. Ensure that you follow the rules to the letter. You do not want to find out what the consequences will be if you deviate.

The King will arrive in Adraga four days before the Thunder Moon has risen". Zi again smiled at Ara, looking at Zale, he raised his hand and disappeared, leaving Zale and Ara looking in amazement at the empty space where he had been standing.

CHAPTER FOURTEEN

Tarrin, Lexi and Conall entered the Kingdom on the morning of the third day after leaving their home. They had made good time having only stopped once to rest and that was for Conall's sake rather than theirs.

As they made their way through the City, they passed through the main marketplace, which as usual was bustling with people. The vendors had set up stalls higgledy-piggledy across the vast square. All kinds of produce and goods were being sold and the smell of hot food and freshly baked bread filled the air.

Tarrin breathed deeply, he had always loved the markets and used to often come with Varick to taste the wares. Tarrin's favourite of all the stalls was the one that sold the apple honey breads. He didn't know why, but he just absolutely loved them.

"Conall, Lexi give me a minute", Tarrin turned his horse and made his way to where the stall used to be. He smiled when he saw it was still there and the lady behind the cart was the same, albeit looking a little bit older. Tarrin jumped of his horse and made his way to the stall.

"Mari", whispered Tarrin with a smile. Mari looked up with a start as she had been pulling more loaves out from her basket under the cart.

"Your Highness", she whispered back, tears filling her eyes. Tarrin had always been her favourite, and she had missed him when he had been banished. Without saying a word, she pulled out a clean muslin cloth, wrapped up six apple honey breads and handed them to Tarrin, who in turn placed a gold coin in her hand.

Mari protested that it was too much, but Tarrin just smiled waiving his hand as he led his horse back to Lexi and Conall.

"We have all missed you Highness", with a little bow Mari turned back to the other customers deflecting attention from Tarrin.

"Let's go I've got what I wanted", Tarrin smiled with a cheeky grin at Lexi.

A short time later they entered the courtyard of the Palace. Conall took all their horses to the stables to be tended, while Tarrin and Lexi made their way into the palace. Some of the palace servants stopped in their tracks when they saw Tarrin, bowing low with huge grins on their faces.

Tarrin and Lexi smiled back as they made their way to the family rooms. At this time of day Tarrin expected Varick to be just breaking his morning fast and Tarrin had brought the apple honey breads for that very reason.

At the threshold of the family rooms Lexi hesitated, "I think Tarrin perhaps I should wait here?", Lexi whispered quietly.

"You will do no such thing, sister-in-law", boomed Varick

from behind. Both Tarrin and Lexi turned with a start as Varick embraced them both.

"It has been too long my brother, I have missed you", Varick hugged his brother tightly. "I am sorry that you have had to come under such circumstances".

As they entered the room, Queen Althea who was already seated, stood up quickly when she saw Tarrin and Lexi.

"Oh, my dear it is so good to see you. You look as gorgeous as ever Lexi", guiding them to the table as she spoke.

"I bring a small gift for you Varick", Tarrin opened up the wrapped apple honey breads which were still warm and passed them round. Biting into his, honey dribbled down his chin. Tarrin moaned with delight as the delicious honey filled his mouth.

"So, tell me Varick, what has been going here, that I find that my son's life is now at stake?"

"I have convened a meeting in the Contemplation Hall in two hours' time. You and Lexi freshen up and meet me there. All involved in the Games will be in attendance including Rebel". Tarrin nodded at Varick and said no more.

They continued to catch up with news as they ate and after they had finished breaking their fast, Tarrin and Lexi made their way to Tarrin's rooms in the palace after agreeing to meet Varick and Althea in the Contemplation Hall once they had freshened up.

Rebel and his team were the first to arrive in the Contemplation Hall. Instructing them all, Rebel asked them to place themselves strategically around the room. In particular, he wanted Drizzle to stand close to the Serpentes Nest and Crick close to Rebel.

"If you hear anything that is spoken against the King from the Serpentes Drizzle, then make sure you let Crick know, so he can forewarn me. The rest of you be on alert, it is of utmost importance that these talks go smoothly". As Rebel finished speaking Storm, Katrina and Librarian Xin walked in. They made their way towards Rebel as they all waited for the King to arrive.

The room filled up as the High Elders of the twelve families arrived. Queen Shahmaran attended as High Elder Manasa for the meeting, as was fitting for the Serpentes Nest.

Rebel started as he saw who was with King Varick when he walked in.

"Father", Rebel rushed to meet Tarrin, whom he hadn't seen for nearly three years, hugging him close. Over his shoulder Rebel saw his mother and grinned widely.

"Ma, what brings you here?", hugging his mother tightly and kissing her on the cheek.

"You do. It seems that you keep getting into trouble, and we keep having to bail you out". Lexi held him tightly tears trickling from the corners of her eyes. "Stop crying Ma, all will be well, trust me". Rebel released her and took his position next to King Varick. Prince Tarrin stood to the right of Varick. He had also worn his gold circlet as a reminder to all present that he was still a Prince of the Realm.

“Has Master Zi not arrived back from Adraga?”, questioned Varick.

“I am here my King”, answered Zi as he walked into the Hall, making his way towards Varick he saw Tarrin standing next to the King.

“Your Highness Prince Tarrin, it is so very good to see you”, smiled Zi as he made a small bow and went to stand beside Rebel.

Rebel had arranged chairs for all who were attending the meeting as well as a table which had been set up for five people at one end of the room, as per King Varick’s instructions.

“Master Zi, Tarrin, Storm and High Elder Manasa, please all take a seat at the table”. Varick also took a seat and faced everyone in the room. Queen Althea, Prince Jai, Princess Sophia, Rebel and Queen Katrina, had all taken a seat on the front row of chairs with the rest taking up the remaining chairs.

Varick was about to start talking when the doors to the Contemplation Hall burst open. In walked Zale of the Thunder Dragons dressed in the armour of his rank as the Leader of the Thunder Dragons.

Zi did not flinch as he knew that Zale could fly fast and was half expecting him to turn up. He had suspected that Zale had a spy in the palace and the fact that he was here for the meeting so quickly, proved it.

Varick stood up quickly, as he saw Rebel and his team making their way towards the intruder having not recognised him.

"Stop Rebel", Varick instructed and then turned to Zale.

"It is good to see you cousin, I was not sure if you would make the journey", Varick spoke, inwardly thinking that Zale would not have missed it for anything.

Zale gave a low bow to Varick, "Cousin once I heard that you needed my help, I did all in my power to make sure I attended", drawled Zale with a sly grin.

"Rebel please place a chair next to yours", indicating to Zale to sit. Varick looked back at the High Elders and started to speak, "Thank you all for gathering here today. As my son Prince Jai has already explained we will now be holding the Dragon Games in the month of the Thunder Moon. I will ask Queen Katrina of the Felinia Clowder to announce the details of the games with the help of Librarian Xin". Varick smiled at Katrina as he spoke.

Some in the room started to grumble and whispers could be heard, "Why are the Felinia Clowder involved they are not of the Twelve?

Looking directly at the person who had whispered the comment Varick boomed across the room, "That is why the Felinia Clowder are involved... BECAUSE they are not of the Twelve and therefore have no vested interest in the games". With that Varick again indicated to Kat and Xin to carry on. The High Elder in question lowered his eyes and went silent in embarrassment at being shouted at by the

King.

"Thank you, your Majesty", Katrina bowed low to King Varick and then turned towards all gathered in the room, making a point of pausing as her eyes met Zale's. Narrowing her eyes slightly as she held Zale's gaze for a few seconds before casting it back to the crowd.

"As King Varick has announced the games will take place during the month of the Thunder Moon. They will start exactly when night finishes and day starts, so we have a full day of light to complete the games. Librarian Xin please could you announce the order of the games and the rules", Katrina nodded to Xin.

Xin looked around him and took a deep breath before he started to speak…
"There will be five elemental games in all.

Each will involve one of the five elements of Water, Wood, Fire, Metal and Earth. The first games will involve the Water Element and will be held in the coastal City of Adraga home to the Thunder Dragons.

The remaining four element games will be held here at Druk Palace at the Gaming Fields". Pausing for a moment Xin looked across the room to see if anyone had any questions. No questions were raised so he continued….

"The two teams within the Dragon Games are Prince Rebel and King Storm against Prince Raulf and Jonas of the Glaring", as Xin took a breath a voice interrupted him...

"There will be a third team", a voice like rumbling thunder made everyone turn to look at the person who had spoken. It was Zale of the Thunder Dragons, who had stood up when he had spoken and towered above those around him. At the same time Rebel had also stood up, in readiness for any potential trouble.

He noted that the rest of his team had also come to attention and were looking at him for instructions. Rebel gave a slight shake of his head and noted that Zale had observed this action with a small grin on his face.

"Do not worry Cousin Varick, I am not here to cause trouble, but to let all here gathered know the intentions of the Thunder Dragons. I have already left instructions for my Guard in Adraga to prepare for the Water Element Games as per Master Zi's instructions", Zale then sat down, a smug look on his face.

Katrina stepped forward and whispered something in Librarian Xin's ear. Librarian Xin again turned to the crowd but this time he looked directly at Zale...

"Leader of the Thunder Dragons, Zale, you have until setting of the sun two days' prior to the full Thunder Moon, to announce your team, otherwise you will forfeit your chance to take part. As there are no other challengers to the games, I will now advise you all of the rules". Xin looked at Katrina for acknowledgement to continue. Katrina nodded and Xin carried on...

"The rules to the games are simple, fight to the death, the surviving pair will be the winners and the lead challenger will be King', Xin finished the last part of the sentence quietly.

At this point Katrina spoke, "The actual games and rules

for each Element will be announced at the time they are to be played. As the first will be in the City of Adraga preparations should be made by all who attend to arrive at Adraga two days before the start of the Water Element Games. Leader Zale, we will await your answer", Kat finished speaking looking towards the King. "Majesty", said Kat sitting back down with Librarian Xin.

CHAPTER FIFTEEN

Jonas looked around the cell he had been in since making the challenge for the Key. The cell was situated in the dungeons below Druk Palace, it was small but clean. Some hay had been placed on one side of the cell, which he lay upon now. He had been treated well; Jonas acknowledged to himself. He particularly welcomed his daily meal of milk and fish which he had not expected as a prisoner of the realm.

His mind was flitting from excitement to guilt to fear and back to excitement. He could not believe that he had made the challenge. When Prince Raulf had first come to him with the idea he had jumped at the chance of becoming leader of the Felinia Clowder.

It had been nearly ten days since he had made the challenge and locked up in the dungeon. The excitement of the challenge had started to wane, as nothing had happened since he had been arrested. He had heard nothing, no one had even told him whether the challenge had been accepted. Also, as he had been treated so well, regret was now the main feeling Jonas had as he was not sure what his fate would be.

As he pondered about the challenge, he heard a door being unlocked further down the dungeons. Jonas could hear footsteps coming closer to where he was being held and stood up to stand by the door of the cell waiting to see who it was. A light filtered through at the end of the corridor as the person holding it turned the corner.

Jonas peered through the cell bars to see who it was. He recognised Rebel and Storm and moved slowly back into his cell awaiting their arrival.

Jonas had heard a lot about Rebel and his team, he also knew that Storm was a part of it. Storm was King of the Felinia Black another faction of the Felinia Clowder. Jonas as leader of the Glaring was becoming very wary that Storm was here as the Felinia Black were renowned for their magical powers.

Jonas could smell Storm approaching. He arched his back in readiness of what was to come, fear was his overwhelming feeling knowing what he knew about Storm.

Rebel and Storm has been instructed by King Varick to allow Jonas to prepare for the games along with Raulf.

Varick, Prince Tarrin and Prince Jai had gone to speak to Raulf to inform him of what had been decided regarding the games. They were all to meet at the Gaming fields in an hours time.

Rebel briefly told Jonas what had transpired since he had made the challenge, whilst Storm had opened the jail door for Jonas to exit. Storm towered above Jonas, his green eyes glittering in the light from the torch. Storm made a low growl in his throat as he stared at Jonas before he turned his back and motioned to Rebel to lead the way out.

Rebel looked at Storm when he growled, recognising it as a warning to Jonas, smiling inwardly to himself. A growl from Storm was indeed a warning to be heeded. He also noted that Jonas had cowered slightly when he heard the growl. This was a good sign indeed.

"Follow me Jonas and no funny business otherwise I'll let Storm loose on you". Rebel looked at Storm as he said this with a twinkle in his eye which Jonas could not see.

Storm frowned and said nothing as they all made their way out of the dungeons and headed towards the Gaming fields with Jonas walking ahead of them.

As they approached the fields, they could see King Varick with Prince Tarrin, Prince Jai and Prince Raulf. Raulf was guarded by Tarrin and Jai. King Varick held the Caysand cloak in his hands. Raulf's aura was now on permanent display with the blue tinge even stronger than it was before.

Rebel allowed his dragon within to flare creating a bright light around him as he approached the group with Storm and Jonas. Tarrin looked at his son eyes widening as he saw the dragon aura around Rebel.

Raulf and Jai also looked at Rebel in amazement, they also had not seen him with an aura. Raulf of course was still unaware that Rebel was his cousin and looked most surprised that Rebel a 'layman' had the capability of having an aura.

Tarrin put his arm across Rebel's shoulder as he came close and whispered, "You look magnificent my son. I did not know you could do this". In response Rebel replied, "Father you only see a small amount of what I am capable of". Rebel spoke loud enough for Raulf to hear, watching him closely for any reaction to what he had just said.

On hearing Rebel call his uncle 'father', Raulf looked towards his own father and brother to see if this was true. He could see by their reaction that they both knew this to be true. Looking back at Rebel, Raulf sized him up, eyes narrowing before looking away into the distance.

Rebel noticed a flicker of something in his eyes before Raulf averted his gaze. Good, Rebel thought he is worried, it was just the reaction Rebel was hoping for.

Rebel turned towards Varick, "Majesty what are your instructions regarding Jonas and Prince Raulf?"

Master Zi spoke, having arrived a few minutes after Rebel, Storm and Jonas. Catching the last few words of what Rebel had just said to Varick.

"If I may your Majesty can I suggest that Prince Raulf and Jonas are left in my care for the duration of the games so that I can ensure that they do not do anything that might jeopardise the event", Zi spoke looking at the group all of whom knew who he was, except of course Raulf and Jonas who were still ignorant of the fact.

"An excellent idea Zi", Varick responded.

"In fact, Master Zi why don't you use the gaming fields as I am sure that Rebel and Storm have already made arrangements for where they will train". Varick was about to continue speaking when Prince Raulf interrupted...

"Father why would a member of the Felinia Clowder be allowed to supervise and instruct me a Royal?", Raulf spoke with indignation.

Varick looked at his eldest son with a mixture of sorrow and disdain, "Raulf you have given up any right to your heritage and therefore everything that goes with it. As far as I am concerned Master Zi, is not only a much better person than you but also the most loyal to the Kingdom. To that end he is also now of higher rank than you". Varick finished cryptically not explaining any further to Raulf what he meant.

Clasping Master Zi's hands Varick whispered quietly into his good ear, "Be careful my Lord, for I do not know how powerful Raulf has become since being underground. I leave you my Caysand Cloak in case you need it", Varick started to hand over the cloak as he finished speaking.

"Keep it my friend, I know exactly how strong Raulf is! Be not afraid Varick all will be well, the Gods have willed it", Zi spoke with a quiet determination for Varick's ears only.

No one else was aware of the interaction between the two as Zi had created an illusion that as far as all the others were concerned Zi was just standing there smiling.

Zi ushered Raulf and Jonas towards the furthest gaming field and told them that they had only two hours a day to train. With that he sat down on the grass crossing his legs, folded his arms and then closed his eyes. Jonas and Raulf just stood there looking at him in amazement.

"Do not assume I cannot see or hear what you are doing just because my eyes are closed, I suggest you do not waste time and continue with your training", Zi spoke commandingly.

Raulf walked towards Zi slowly flaring his blue aura in the hope of catching Zi with it. Suddenly, a bright white light encompassed Zi which made Raulf stop in his tracks unsure of what it meant. Raulf stood there for a few minutes thinking about what to do next, when the white aura around Zi started to grow. As it reached Raulf's blue aura, Zi's white aura started to absorb the blue that surrounded Raulf. Raulf let out a loud scream as the pain was so intense that he moved back quickly away from the white aura.

"If you've learnt your lesson Raulf, I suggest you continue with your training", Zi drawled slowly, still with his eyes closed. This time however a small smile had reached his lips.

Jonas had watched the entire interaction and was now shaking with fear of what not only Raulf could do but also Zi. Jonas knew he was in big trouble, but he had no idea how to get out of it as he was in so deep. He also had no idea that Zi was so powerful, no wonder I couldn't defeat him thought Jonas to himself, wishing even more that he had not made the challenge or agreed to work with Raulf.

Raulf had gone pale in the face, totally shocked at what had happened. He had not in his wildest dreams expected that someone from the Felinia Clowder could be more powerful than himself. He had learnt this lesson the hard way and started to back away from Zi. Once he reached Jonas, he motioned him to move further away from Zi and whispered quietly… "I think we should plan carefully Jonas if we are to achieve what we set out to do".

Jonas nodded his head slowly fear showing clearly on his face, "Yes my Prince", going silent waiting for Raulf to continue.

Storm, Varick, Tarrin and Rebel made their way back to the palace when Rebel turned towards his father,

"Father we need to speak to you, your Majesty too as a matter of urgency?", looking at Storm at the same time.

"Is everything alright my son?" Tarrin responded quickly.

"Yes father, everything will be alright, which is why I need to talk to you all", replied Rebel cryptically.

"Storm it would also be helpful if Katrina can join us. Please could you find her and meet us in the Contemplation Hall", with that Rebel, his father and King Varick who looked at his brother with a wry smile at the way Rebel had taken over, made their way towards the Contemplation Hall.

The palace was bustling with activity, no doubt in anticipation of the games thought Varick to himself. He hoped he had made the right decision in agreeing to the Dragon Games. The cost would be high, either he would lose a son or his brother Tarrin would. This thought kept crossing Varick's mind, his heart already feeling heavy with what was to come.

"Brother, I know what plays on your mind", spoke Tarrin quietly to Varick so no one else could hear... "It plays on mine too, but I trust you and know that you would have made the decision for the good of the Kingdom. If it means we must lose a son for the Kingdom to survive, then so be it. I am with you Varick, I always have been". Tarrin placed his right arm over Varick's shoulders in a brotherly gesture as they entered the palace.

As they arrived at the Contemplation Hall, they made their way to the antechamber. Storm and Katrina entered the room just as they were taking their seats.

"Okay we are all here", spoke Rebel

"Katrina, please could you explain to all present what happened when I was with you and Storm in The Valley of the Five", Rebel requested.

Kat looked at Rebel, then at everybody sitting at the table.

"It was most extraordinary what Rebel was able to do. His magic is the most powerful I have ever seen. So much so I am not sure exactly how powerful Rebel is!", finished Kat looking at Rebel with a small smile on her face.

"I think Storm and I should be able to defeat Raulf and Jonas father', Rebel spoke to Tarrin looking at Storm for confirmation.

"Son, this is good news, but I hope you do not forget that if you win, Raulf will forfeit his life. Not only that, there may be another contender in Zale of the Thunder Dragons, who is renowned for his prowess in the Water Element Games. Also, do not forget that death is a consequence of the Dragon Games which is why they were changed to the Games of Shengxiao by the Gods", Tarrin spoke softly, his voice tinged with sadness.

"Rebel", interrupted Storm, "I am pretty sure that Zale with his partner, will be a big challenge for us in the Water Element games as that is the favoured element for the Thunder Dragons", spoke Storm with caution.

King Varick held up his hand, indicating to everyone to stop speaking,

"Tarrin spoke true Rebel, one of us will lose a son in these games no matter what the outcome, however, if Zale wins then that would mean we lose you both. That is not acceptable. We must plan well for the games so that we can have an outcome which would favour the Ledary Dragons.

To that end, Storm and Kat I need you both to work together with Rebel to fully prepare him for the challenges of the Water Element Games. I know that you both have knowledge of the original Dragon Games and what is involved in all the Elements of the Games".

As has been identified the Water Element games will challenge us the most as it is favoured by the Thunder Dragons. So, work with Rebel on this Element first, make your way to my home on the coast of Adraga where you will be able to practice in peace with no watchful eyes.

We will meet you there four days, before the Water Element Games start. This will also allow us to prepare before the rest of the families arrive so we can go over the strategy. In the meantime, we will make preparations for the other Element Games here in Druk, in readiness for when you return hopefully as victors of the Water Element games.

"You are right my Liege we will leave today for Adraga",

Kat spoke sombrely looking at Storm and Rebel.

“Perhaps Uncle, we could also take my team so that we can ensure that the preparations for the Water Games go as planned”, asked Rebel.

“A very good idea Rebel, who were you thinking of taking with you?”, Varick responded.

“I was thinking Mercy, Drizzle and Keon. We shall leave Crick behind so that we have a way of communicating quickly if necessary”, finished Rebel.

“Good, do that Rebel lad and be careful all of you, the fate of the Kingdom rests on your shoulders Rebel. I know also you will do all you can to ensure success”. Varick stood up as he finished speaking signalling to them all that the meeting was now over.

Varick went across to Rebel and hugged him, “I know that this will be a difficult task for you, but also know that if at any point during a life and death situation between yourself and Raulf, save yourself lad, you have done nothing wrong you should not be the one to suffer. Raulf has brought this upon himself, I blame him for the situation we are all in”. Varick made his way to the door closing it behind him slowly as he left the room.

Tarrin turned to his son, “Sit Rebel, we will work out a game plan now”, Tarrin as General of the Sheng Army was a master strategist, that made him the ideal person to help with the preparations of the games.

Varick made his way to where his Queen Althea was planning the organisation of the games. She had decided to use the palace dining area as her base as it had lots of tables and a ready supply of food for all who were involved. As he entered the dining room, he could see a hive of activity with Althea right in the thick of it as she gave instructions to various members of staff.

To one side of her, High Elder Manasa was stood giving Althea her support by just being there but doing little. Shaking his head slightly a small smile on his face, he caught Manasa's attention indicating to a table by the window which was not being used.

Manasa in her true form was Queen Shahmaran of the Serpentes, Varick needed Manasa to be Shahmaran during the games. Varick knew he could do with all the help he could muster, during the Dragon Games, in particular, the Water Element Games.

Varick also knew, that Raulf had committed a grievous sin against the Serpentes when he had murdered some of the Serpentes in the Temple of Shahmaran. Shahmaran herself would not let Raulf get away with this, death would be her punishment for Raulf. He needed her to back down on this if the games were to be fair.

"King Varick how can I be of service", Manasa lisped gently. Varick had always liked Manasa with her gentle ways. He hoped he could win her over.

"Queen Shahmaran I have a request. I do not ask this lightly as I am fully aware of the sins that have been committed to the Serpentes Nest by Raulf. I know that you also rule the serpents of the sea. The first Element of the games to be played is Water. The location for the Water Games as you know is Adraga. I think you would agree that it is imperative that the Ledary Dragon Clan win the Games and the Key. For if the Thunder Dragons win then the whole of the Kingdom of Shengxiao will be in turmoil". Varick paused, giving Shahmaran a considering look, before continuing...

"I have every confidence in Rebel and Storm in defeating Raul and Jonas, however the Water Games traditionally have always been won by the Thunder Dragons. Your help in us achieving a win in this element would be much appreciated.

I only ask for advice on knowledge of the sea that may assist Rebel in this element. What say you Manasa, will you be able to assist us in this?" Varick had spoken matter of factly looking at Manasa questioningly.

Manasa stared back with no indication of what she was thinking on her face. Varick could see that she was pondering about her response and stayed quiet until she was ready to speak. A full twenty minutes had passed before she finally spoke...

"I have one caveat your Highness, which you must agree to if I am to help you", lisped Manasa quietly.

"Speak Manasa", Varick nodding his agreement to the caveat before he had even heard it.

"No matter who wins the games Varick, Raulf will be mine at the end to do with as I will no questions asked", Manasa spoke resolutely.

Varick looked at her as he contemplated on what she had

said… “Agreed”, uttered Varick. Standing up he gave a quick nod to Manasa before leaving.

CHAPTER SIXTEEN

The Kings Palace as it was known in Adraga shone brightly in the midday sun; it was also made from Caysand and it was magnificent in its splendour. Totally different in style from the palace in Shengxiao it sprawled across the cliff tops low and long with huge landing platforms built into the walls for easy access.

Rebel had already sent his team ahead of him, only Storm and Katrina were with him as they rode along the edge of the Cliffs of Adraga towards the Palace.

The journey to Adraga had thankfully been uneventful, and they had all had an opportunity to discuss the Water Element games. As they approached the Palace, Rebel was now confident that he could win this challenge.

The cliff road to the Palace was long and narrow which made the going slow with the horses treading carefully as they were becoming quite jittery. The wind had picked up and buffeted them dangerously as they made their way slowly to the palace which was still a league away.

"Storm, Katrina I will change into dragon and meet you there". Rebel was now shouting above the wind which had started to howl around them. They both nodded as Rebel rose above them in his dragon form.

To their utter amazement Rebel was a white dragon, his scales were tipped with gold, he was magnificent. They looked at each other, surprise written on both of their faces.

"Did you know Storm? Did you know he was the Dragon-gold?", gasped Katrina

"I did not?", Storm shouted the words which were being whipped out of his mouth by the wind.

"No dear, but I think we should also transform, we will get to the palace a lot quicker as something is not quite right about this wind it feels very ominous to me". Katrina and Storm both jumped of their horses as Katrina whispered to the horses quickly before they galloped off towards the direction of the palace.

Storm was a Mobay, his coat solid black in colour, sleek and shiny. Green eyes looked at Katrina and Storm purred in pleasure as he stared into his wife's blue eyes. Katrina was beautiful, with white silky hair on her body, with black ears, paws, tail and face she hailed from a land far away called Jacana.

Katrina stuck out her pink tongue as she turned, running quickly in the direction of the palace. Storm followed behind Katrina staying close to her, a sign of protection and love.

As they approached the palace Katrina mind melded with Storm exclaiming, "Honey look at the sea!" Storm turned his head towards the sea and meowed loudly... "Quickly Kat to the Palace". Storm stared a second longer towards the sea, and then they both fled for the safety of the palace.

The sea had gone wild, never had they seen it like this. The waves were enormous crashing onto the beach. Out into the distance a wave like no other was gathering speed, towering at least half a league high and stretched two leagues long. The water was inky black in colour and the sky so dark that it was hard to distinguish where the water stopped, and the sky started. Lightening flashed indiscriminately creating a maelstrom of streaking light as the wind whipped even faster around them.

It was a frightening sight and it was heading towards the palace. They must warn all at the palace so they could evacuate before the wave struck.

As they were a few feet from the palace gates they both transformed back to their human forms.

"OPEN THE GATES", bellowed Storm, "QUICKLY MAN".

As they ran in, Rebel came running towards them having heard Storm's shout, "What is it Storm?", "Rebel look at the sea", shouted Katrina.

Rebel looked through the gates and out towards the sea, "It's magic Katrina I can see a red aura around it, somebody is doing this", he exclaimed as he ran towards one of the platforms near the gates. Storm had matched Rebel step for step, both climbed the wide ladder quickly, Storm being faster as he was Felinia. By the time they reached the middle of the platform Rebel was dragon taking flight. Quickly he winged his way towardsthe sea. The huge wave was getting closer and closer, it was now nearly a league high above the sea.

"Rebel what are you going to do?", Katrina asked via mind meld.

"Katrina stay linked I may need your help", responded Rebel turning his head to give a quick look towards Katrina and Storm as he climbed higher into the sky.

Katrina raised her hand in acknowledgment clasping Storms hands pulling him down onto the platform into a kneeling position. "Close your eyes Storm, Rebel may need both of us to combat this".

Rebel could clearly see where the aura was originating from and headed in its direction. The wind was wild and squally making it difficult for Rebel to fly as it pushed against him as if knowing that it needed to stop him. Rebel streamlined himself like an arrow with a quick strong whip of his wings he pulled them close to his side and aimed himself directly towards where the aura was originating.

The red aura was emanating just below the surface of the water a hundred feet in front of the wave and it streaked the full length of the wave as if driving it along. As Rebel entered the water, he could see what looked like a thunder dragon moving fast along the length of the wave, with its tail long and flat rather than pointed it undulated quickly making the dragon move extremely fast in the water.

As he sped towards the creature Rebel flared his aura and allowed it to streak across the sea matching the red aura in length, he followed closely behind the thunder dragon who had sped up as it realised what Rebel was doing.

someone. Rebel sped up landing near the edge of the platform he quickly transformed back to his human form. Moving quickly towards Storm he realised it was Katrina lying unconscious on the floor.

“Storm what happened?”, Rebel shouted, as he knelt down beside Katrina holding one of her hands in his.

“She collapsed soon after you tapped into her energy, she wasn’t ready when you took it lad, you must help her now”, Storm’s voice broke on the last word.

“Storm I need you to move back from Katrina make sure you are not touching her in any way”, instructed Rebel as he positioned himself cross-legged behind Katrina’s head. He placed both hands on either side of Katrina’s head, covering her ears. Closing his eyes, he lowered his head until it touched forehead to forehead with Katrina.

Storm looked on anxiously, a long time had passed since Rebel had gone into his trance. Storm was becoming genuinely concerned; however, he still did not touch Katrina or disturb Rebel. He knew that what Rebel was doing was a first, there had not been a dragon healer born in centuries until Rebel.

Storm hoped Rebel knew what he was doing reassuring himself at the same time, that he was sure Rebel would know. Still he fidgeted where he sat as he looked at one, then the other constantly looking for some sign that all would be well.

It was well into the night when Storm saw Katrina’s eyes flicker open. Rebel lifted his head slowly and leaned back lowering himself down onto the platform his eyes still closed. Storm jumped up taking a huge step towards Katrina, lifting her slowly he cradled her in his arms.

It was only then that Storm looked up with any kind of awareness as he had been so focused on Rebel and Katrina. At some point during the night a full guard of soldiers holding lit torches had surrounded them. Among them stood Mercy, Drizzle and Keon looking on anxiously. Mercy had started to run towards Rebel as he lay there with his eyes closed.

"Rebel, Rebel are you okay?" Mercy whispered sobbing into his ear. Rebel opened his eyes slowly… "Mercy I need water, please bring me some water". Mercy shouted out to anyone listening, "Water bring water… NOW", she shouted between sobs.

A soldier handed Mercy a cup full of water, "Rebel, Rebel, here drink", Mercy whispered as she lifted Rebel's head up slightly putting the cup to his lips. Rebel drank slowly at first then gulped it down, "More Mercy!", rasped Rebel.

The guard filled the cup full again quickly with Rebel drinking it just as quickly, "Fill it again man and give some to Katrina, she will need it also", spoke Rebel between gulps. On hearing this Storm motioned for someone to give him a cup of water and started to give small sips to Katrina.

Rebel was on his fifth cup when he finally spoke, "Mercy make arrangements to take Katrina to her rooms in the palace, Storm go with them, I will follow shortly". Turning to the guards, "Who is in charge among you?" questioned Rebel.

"I am sir, Tomo", spoke a burly looking man.

"Tomo, I need you to place guards around the palace and close the palace gates immediately. Keon, please assist Tomo, once you have done this report back to me in my rooms", Rebel had stood up with help from Mercy, as he gave the instructions and started to slowly make his way to the steps of the platform.

"Drizzle, please come with me I need to send a message to King Varick and my father", with that they slowly headed towards the palace, Drizzle keeping pace with Rebel who was walking slowly due to the effects of the healing magic he had just performed.

From the vantage point of his cave high above the cliffs of Adraga, Zale stood staring out to sea a frown marring his face. He knew Wyetta was dead, it was an unexpected turn of events. He had been shocked to see a Dragongold. Legends had been written about the Dragongold, the stories were told to all the young dragons at school, but never had one been seen before, either in his lifetime or many hundreds of years before that.

It was magnificent, Zale had been awed by its majestic beauty as it dived into the sea. Zale also knew at that moment that Wyetta would be in serious trouble.

Wyetta had been the most powerful thunder dragon in his clan, her skills in working magical spells was second to none, especially the ability to control water like no other dragon he knew, except now. Zale had been very close to Wyetta, although he had never formally tied a bond with her, they had had a child together. Zale silently mourned her death and with a heavy heart he knew he had to break the news of Wyetta's death to their daughter Ara.

Zale had advised Wyetta against this, but she had not listened, insisting that she could give Zale a head start by eliminating one off his opponents before the games had even begun. He also knew that he was now at a huge disadvantage with a Dragongold it was going to be near impossible to win the Water Element games.

Zale turned suddenly and made his way towards his daughter Ara's room. As he walked Zale's thoughts went to when Ara was born. He had not been present at her birth in fact he was not even aware that Wyetta had been carrying his child. Now he had to break it to Ara that her mother was dead. He slowed his steps standing still outside the entrance of his daughter's room. A white silk sheet blowing gently in the breeze which filtered through the cave, covered the entrance.

"Father I know you are there you may come in" a small sobbing voice spoke to Zale.

Zale entered slowly, continually amazed at his daughter's awareness skills. Ara was lying on her bed looking up at the ceiling of the cave. Her eyes were blotchy and red tears still trickling down her face. "Mother's dead isn't she?" sobbed Ara.

Zale was shocked that Ara already knew, "How?", whispered Zale.

"Father we never told you this, mother and I were bondlinked. Everything she went through I experienced too and-vice-versa. I know exactly what mother went through just now and at what point she lost her life. She sent a message for you father", Ara looked at Zale her small face turned towards him with her big beautiful round eyes full of tears she beckoned Zale over to her.

Zale knelt down next to her bed and held her hands, "What did she say Ara?",

"Mother said that the Dragongold was the most powerful dragon she had ever come across. Mother tells of a legend which has been foretold that to beat a Dragongold you would need a sword that had been forged from the Caysand which is then etched with the markings of the five earthly elements. Then she said she loves you father and loves me too", with that Ara started to sob again. Zale pulled her close into his arms hugging her tight, tears rolled down his eyes, the loss of Wyetta even more stark with Ara in his arms.

The games had now become personal, he swore to himself, he would do whatever it takes to beat Rebel and Raulf to gain the Crown and the Kingdom. Wyetta's death would not be in vain.

Rebel mind linked with Varick and his father Tarrin with Drizzle as the go between. Rebel quickly relayed what had occurred leaving out no details. He could feel the anger rising in both his father and King Varick's mind as they listened to what he was saying.

After he finished speaking there was silence, it lasted so long he looked at Drizzle questioningly asking via mindmeld... "Drizzle is the link still there?"

"Yes, we are still here son", responded Tarrin.

"This is unprecedented that the Thunder dragons would do this. We will speak with Master Zi about this and inform you of what we learn as soon as we can. Look after yourself son", finished Tarrin.

"Yes, yes and please convey our thoughts to Katrina, I hope she has no ill effects remaining from her experience. You have performed the very first magical dragon healing that we have ever heard of Rebel. Especially as the healing was for someone not of your family origin. It's truly amazing, amazing…", Varick's voice faded away as Drizzle closed off the mind-meld, looking at Rebel with renewed respect.

"Stop looking at me like that Drizzle it was nothing, please go get me some more drink with some food, and make sure extra goes to Katrina too, she will need it to recover", then Rebel turned towards the small room off his bedchamber where a huge bath sat in the middle of the room full of hot water. Beside the bath on a small stool was some soap and a small cloth to wash himself with.

Rebel undressed quickly and lowered himself slowly into the hot water, gasping at the initial burn from the heat. Rebel was frozen cold and so tired after the day's events that he washed himself quickly getting out of the bath as soon as he was done patting himself dry as he entered his bedchamber. A set of clean clothes had been placed on his bed and he put them on quickly. As he was finishing fastening his shirt, Drizzle walked back in with a servant following close behind carrying a tray laden with steaming hot food and drink.

Rebel's stomach rumbled with hunger, as he realised, he had not eaten since the day before. He sat at the table where the food had been placed mumbling his thanks as he tore piece of bread from a steaming loaf and dipped it into the meaty gravy which surrounded a platter laden with beef and vegetables. Moaning with pleasure Rebel did not speak again until most of the food on the tray had gone. Picking up a tankard full of ale he took huge gulps and only stopped once it was empty.

Rebel sat back in his chair and closed his eyes. Only one image running through his mind, that of the female thunder dragon motionless deep within the sea, her long hair billowing gently around her beautiful face.

Rebel reached out to Kat… "Kat I'm going to tap into your power so I can stop this thing". Without waiting for Kat to respond Rebel started to flare his aura even brighter using up his energy and tapping into Kats.

Rebel's aura flared so bright it lit up the sea for miles around encompassing and extinguishing the red aura as if he were snuffing out a candle. The thunder dragon screamed loudly in sheer pain that Rebel struggled to maintain his control as he watched the thunder dragon writhe and thrash around in the water.

As he looked, he could see that the thrashing and movement was getting slower when suddenly, the thunder dragon stopped moving. It had taken a good five minutes for this to happen. Rebel was exhausted both mentally and physically.

He swam towards the motionless figure slowly to check if it was in fact dead. The thunder dragon he realised had changed back to its human form. As he got closer, he realised the thunder dragon was a female. A gold anklet was on her left leg, her long dark hair floated around her head and face with the movement of the water. She was stunningly beautiful, a tinge of sadness and regret filled Rebel as he stared at her.

With a shake of his head, Rebel looked at her for a moment longer before heading to the surface of the water, as he exited the water, he could see the huge wave come crashing down slowly. Rebel managed to free himself from the water aiming high into the sky.

Rebel turned flapping his wings strongly he headed back towards the palace. As he neared the platform where he had left Storm and Katrina, he could see Storm kneeling over

CHAPTER SEVENTEEN

Varick after speaking with Rebel had immediately called a meeting with Master Zi, Queen Shahmaran, Librarian Xin, Crick and Tarrin. They were all now sat around the table in the antechamber of the Contemplation Hall. Tarrin had just finished relaying what had happened in Adraga and all of them sat in silence shocked at what they had heard.

All of them except Queen Shahmaran, "I was expecting something like this may happen", she lisped quietly. "The only thunder dragon that had the magical ability to do this is Wyetta", she looked at Varick as she spoke.

"Wyetta was the mother of Ara, who is the only daughter of Zale, Leader of the Thunder dragons", pausing for a few minutes to let this information sink in with the others, she continued, "With Wyetta dead, we now have another problem on our hands.

Anyone who dies and is bond-linked, all knowledge and skills that belonged to the person who died will pass onto the person to whom they were linked with. This means Ara, daughter of Zale is now the most powerful wielder of magic within the Thunder dragons. She can now bond-link with someone of her own choosing, such is the power of the magic of those who are bond-linked", finished Shahmaran with small hiss.

"We now have three very powerful contenders for the

games assuming that Ara will bond-link with Zale. Raulf's power with his blue aura and Rebel a Dragongold. We must prepare with care if we wish the Kingdom to remain with the Ledary Dynasty. In particular, we would wish that Rebel is the victor and not Raulf", summarised Zi slowly, knowing that this was what everyone was thinking.

"Librarian Xin, please find out everything you can about bond-linked dragons and their strengths. I would also like to know more about the Dragongold. We must have all information at hand to help Rebel succeed in the games. I am sure that Raulf and Zale will be doing the same. Every advantage we can gain will be a bonus when the games begin", Zi commanded Xin, acknowledging Varick's nod of approval as he finished speaking.

Librarian Xin stood up from the table and bowed low, "I will return by midday tomorrow with the information requested your Highnesses", with that he left the room quietly closing the door behind him.

"We will leave for Adraga the day after tomorrow three days before we were due to leave", Varick instructed all at the table.

"Crick, please relay this message to all who need to know so that preparations can be made. Please also inform your brother Drizzle so that he can relay what has been discussed at this meeting to Rebel, Storm and Katrina", Varick then stood up indicating to Tarrin to follow him.

Master Zi and Queen Shahmaran sat there and looked at each other, "I suppose this as good a time as any to discuss that which we have ignored for a very long time my dear

Shahmaran", Zi looked at Shahmaran warmly with a twinkle in his eye.

Shahmaran lowered her eyes hiding what she was thinking from Zi. She had loved him a very long time but had not the courage to tell him about it. She still did not know if she could speak of it.

"Manasa", Zi whispered quietly using her High Elder name as he preferred it.

"Manasa, look at me please". Manasa lifted her eyes slowly and stared into Zi's eyes.

"I have missed you very much, it was only when you left that I realised how much you mean to me. Two hundred years have passed since you left, my feelings for you have grown to the point that I must ask you if you feel the same". Zi had taken hold of her hands as he spoke gently holding them to his chest.

A tear trickled down Manasa's cheek, lowering her eyes once more, "I do Zi, it is one of the reasons that I left and resided on earth for so long. Why do you raise this now, with the Dragon Games looming ahead of us Zi?"

"It is for that very reason that I have raised it. If we are unsuccessful in saving the Kingdom of Shengxiao then I don't want to go into the games without you knowing how much you mean to me. The consequences of the Ledary dragons not winning is not worth contemplating as even as Gods we cannot know what would happen. Even though we should not interfere with what happens on Earth, we may have to. I know that Varick has asked you to speak to the sea serpents what have you decided?" Zi faced her, a serious questioning look in his eyes.

"I will help him; I have already promised him this. As a forfeit he will hand over to me Raulf, if he survives". Manasa spoke with steely determination, "I will have vengeance for what Raulf has done to my people".

Zi nodded slowly, "Yes, yes I understand", he whispered quietly and then gently kissed Manasa on the cheek. "We will talk further my dear, but for now I must go to the Heavenly Palace to speak with the Council of the Omni", standing up Zi kissed Manasa gently on the lips then walked out of the room quietly.

Zi pondered on the situation, Rebel a Dragongold, Raulf a Blue Aura Dragon and now Zale potentially a bond-linked dragon. The games were going to be exciting, challenging and very dangerous he thought to himself as he made his way to the Contemplation Hall.

Zi had to go to the Heavenly Palace to appraise the Council of the Omni of the situation on Earth and that the Dragon Games would now be held instead of the Shengxiao Games. Zi activated the portal to the gates, as he did so he sat in the middle of the circle and whispered one word, ... "Omniscient". With a blink of the eye he disappeared and found himself in his rooms in the Heavenly Palace.

He was not looking forward to the Council meeting as he knew at least three of the twelve who made up the Council would challenge him and vote against the Dragon Games. He thought about the Gods of the third Trine who represented the Panthera, Equidae and Canis families. This Trine had always been the most difficult. However, they only needed a majority and Zi was sure that the others would vote in favour.

Unknown to King Varick the Gods could overrule the decision for the Dragon Games to replace the Shengxiao Games. Zi knew this was not an option, so he prepared his thoughts as he changed his clothes in readiness for the Council meeting which he had arranged as soon as he was aware that the Dragon Games would be played.

Zi was the thirteenth member and the Supreme Leader of the Council. He was of the Felinia Family and the oldest of the Council. Few had ever challenged him as he was revered within the Heavenly Palace. He now hoped that this would work in his favour.

Zi glanced around the Council chamber as he walked in. He had always found great pleasure when he was in the chamber. It was splendid he thought to himself as he looked around at the varieties of flora and fauna of all colours which suited the requirements of all on the Council of Omni.

Seating had been placed all around the chamber and at various levels either on the floor, in the trees or on the walls surrounding the chamber itself. As he looked around Zi could see various members of the council having already taking their preferred seating positions.

There was no requirement for them to be either in the animal form or human, Zi himself had decided to attend in his animal form.

Zi was a magnificent Felinia from the Ankara family. Renowned for their long silky soft white hair. Zi was also unusual as his eyes were different colours too. His left eye was blue in colour and his right brown. This was extremely rare in a cat and as a consequence of his blue eye, Zi was deaf in his left ear.

He was known as a wise and strong leader having led the Omni Council for many years. He was hoping that today of all days the council would take his side. He made his way to his seat which was a huge silky cushion made of white silk with gold threads running through it. Suddenly, he could hear loud gasps around the room, turning around to see what had caused this Zi also stopped in his tracks letting out a slow long purr.

Manasa had entered the room in her snake form, which she had never done before. She looked stunningly beautiful. Zi drew in a deep breath through his nose the scent of jasmine was overpowering, all knew that this was the chosen scent of Shahmaran, God Queen of the Serpentes.

Manasa moved slowly across the room to a large basket near where Zi sat curled upon his cushion. As she passed him, she lisped quietly, "Only for you Zi we must deal with this quickly and get back to Earth" as she slid onto her basket and coiled round making herself comfortable.

Zi acknowledge what she said before turning around to look around the room, all were in attendance. He noted that the Third Trine had all attended in their animal form of a Panthera, Equidae and Canis. They were all sat close together and Zi could see by their body language that there was dissention amongst the Third Trine.

"Thank you all for attending… I will be brief", spoke Zi commandingly. All had quietened in the room and were looking expectantly at him.

"For the benefit of those of you who are not aware of the situation on Earth, I will give you all a short explanation so that you may make an informed decision for what I am about to ask". Zi continued for the next hour relaying what had occurred on Earth over the last few weeks.

Zi paused as he finished taking a deep breath, he looked quickly at Manasa who gave a slight nod of her head. Relieved Zi knew that the Second Trine would vote in favour. He knew that the First Trine would vote in favour too as the Dragonian and Ratticus clans formed part of this. It was the vote of the Fourth Trine he needed which consisted of the Leporidae, Bovidae and Suidae families.

Zi turned first to the First Trine, "What say you families of the First Trine?"

Chenshi God of the Dragonians stool up. Chenshi was a magnificent dragon, like Rebel he was a Dragongold, the only difference was that he had magnificent gold tipped wings and tail that curled and glistened with gold all along its back. Chenshi was fully aware of what was unfolding on Earth and was eager to get this meeting finished.

Bowing low in deference to Zi, Chenshi spoke his voice booming loud around the chamber, "The First Trine vote in favour of the Dragon Games Supreme Leader". When he did finally lift his head up, he glanced around the room quickly before finally sitting back down.

"Shahmaran Queen of the Serpentes, what have the Second Trine decided?", Zi turned to look at Manasa a warmth in his eyes meant only for her.

“Supreme Leader we are in agreement with the First Trine and support this decision fully”, Manasa lissped quietly. As she was settling back down on her seat, she turned to look at the Fourth Trine, her tongue flicked in and out of her mouth quickly a subtle warning to them.

The Fourth Trine had always been scared of the Serpentes and the Leader of the Trine, Weishi of the Bovidae Family looked away quickly, fear flitting across his face.

“Thank you Shahmaran”, Zi looked across the room towards the Third Trine about to ask the same question when a member of the Third Trine interrupted quickly…

“Supreme Leader we will save you the time of asking the question as our decision is NO we do not agree”, It was Yinshi of the Panthera Family who answered and not Wushi who was the Leader of the Trine.

Wushi spoke angrily “Yinshi, you do not speak for all of the Third Trine, only you are against the Dragon Games and we know why. You have never got over the fact that your daughter, Lexi, married Prince Tarrin of the Dragonians against your will. However, this will not affect our decision as I and Xushi of the Canis Families agree with Supreme Leader Zi, and as Leader of the Third Trine my decision is final”, Wushi then turned to address Zi…

“Supreme Leader Tai Sui, the Third Trine are with you in this”. As Wushi finished speaking Yinshi jumped up and arched his back growling under his breath… “You will regret this Wushi”. Yinshi crouched back and jumped twenty feet across the room to the entrance. Turning back Yinshi addressed all in the room,

“You will all regret this, the Panthera Family will not sit back and allow this to happen”, growling angrily, he then leapt out of the room.

The chamber erupted all speaking at once at the audacity of the Yinshi.

“Please everyone let us focus on what is at hand”, boomed Zi turning his attention back to the Fourth Trine.

“What is the decision of the Fourth Trine”, Zi said looking at Weishi of the Bovidae Family.

Weishi looked towards Manasa shaking a little with fear.

“Supreme Leader we have one request before we agree with the games”. Weishi spoke hesitantly fear evident in his voice.

“Speak Weishi of the Bovidae what is it that you request?”, Zi asked gently

“As you know the Families of our Trine have always lived in fear of the Serpentes Family. In particular, the Leporidae Family, who have lost many family members to the Serpentes who feed on them”. Weishi took a quick look at Manasa before flicking his eyes nervously back to Zi.

“Yes, I have been aware of this, it is the nature of the world that those most powerful will overpower the weak”, Zi spoke sombrely nodding to Weishi to continue.

“We would like your assurance Supreme Leader, that this

will not happen in the future as the Leporidae Family have suffered much because of this', finished Weishi a quiver in his voice as he heard Manasa hiss loudly as he finished.

"Shahmaran", Zi spoke looking at Manasa, "From this day forward it is forbidden for the Serpentes Nest to harm any of the family members of the Leporidae". Zi's eyes pleaded with Manasa to agree to this as time was now of the essence and he needed the Fourth Trine to vote in favour.

Manasa flicked her tongue in and out for a few minutes looking at Zi, before she finally turned to Weishi.

"I will agree only to this Weishi of the Bovidae, the Leporidae Family will have a reprieve of one hundred years only. Then we will revert back to the natural order of things, do you agree?", Manasa finished with a hisssss and looked back at Zi with an expression on her face saying this is the only compromise I will make.

"Well Weishi do you agree?", Zi repeated the question, tension in the air as Maoshi of the Leporidae stood up in his human form. He looked at Weishi nodding before announcing…

"The Fourth Trine agree to this", and with that Maoshi bowed low to Manasa and then to Zi before leaving the Chamber.

Zi stood up relieved he got the answer he needed with the backing of the Omni Council. There was no time to be lost. Looking at Manasa he said, "Let us go, as you said there is much to be done", with that Zi changed to his human form and made his way out of the chamber quickly.

CHAPTER EIGHTEEN

King Varick with Prince Tarrin led the way along the coastal road of Adraga towards The Kings Palace. A long entourage followed behind them consisting of their wives, Princess Sofia and her fiancé, High Lord Sylvest, Librarian Xin, Prince Raulf and Jonas. Accompanying all of them were a contingency of the Kings Guard along with the Queens Warrior Maids.

Raulf and Jonas had been locked in a carriage, which was guarded by a mixture of a dozen Kings Guard and Warrior Maids.

They made their way slowly towards the palace, as Tarrin looked out towards the sea he breathed in deeply, tasting the sea salt in the air before turning to speak to Varick, "Brother have your deliberations brought you any answers regarding how the games will be played?", Tarrin asked curiously as he knew that this was a totally new area for Varick and one that he was happy to advise on as he did in the past as the General of the Shengxiao Army.

Tarrin looked at his brother keenly waiting for an answer. Varick hesitated before responding quietly, "You know Tarrin I have missed you greatly over the years you have been away, it is good to have you by my side now. In answer to your question this is the situation currently", pausing to gather his thoughts Varick slowly started to relay what was playing on his mind.

"We have three teams who are all excellent contenders. Rebel a Dragongold with Storm as his partner. Storm who is King of the Felinia Black and advisor to the Gods is a very talented contender in his own right. We have Prince Raulf, a blue aura dragon who has had exposure to the Flamecore, which has made him very powerful. As yet we do not know how powerful he is. His partner Jonas, however, should cause little problem. Finally, we have Zale Leader of the Thunder Dragons, a strong contender too, particularly for the Water Element Games. Also, if Katrina is right in what she said, that his daughter Ara will bond-link with him, then this is an unknown force too.

So, you can see brother the Dragon Games in other circumstances would be something to look forward too with immense anticipation. However, sadly with our two sons pitting against each other we both face very grim decisions to make as to what the final outcome of the Games will be. To this end," continued Varick, "I have decided that we should have a 'Judgement' what say you brother?"

Tarrin looked at Varick in shock, "Are you sure brother? I cannot recall the last time we had a 'Judgement'; it is unheard of in our times", finished Tarrin shock still evident on his face.

Both brothers went silent, 'Judgement' no doubt in the forefront of their minds…

'Judgement' was the ultimate court formed by the Gods of Omni as only they could issue a divine punishment.

"Varick do you not think that a 'Judgement', may be too harsh. Remember, we both have sons in the games and I do not think either one of us would wish a 'Judgement', on either of our sons?" Tarrin spoke softly, as the wind from the sea had picked up and their voices were being carried further down the line.

"It is for that reason I think we should do this. It will be Raulf who will, I believe be the one who tries to cheat at the expense of all so that he may win. I must harden my heart to do what is best for the Kingdom". Varick looked at Tarrin with a finality in his words that brooked no argument.

Tarrin went silent again, a frown marring his brow. He knew his brother meant well, but he also knew that Varick and Althea would be devastated if Raulf was to risk "Judgement". He would speak with Master Zi when next they met, he thought to himself.

The sun was setting as they finally arrived at the Palace of Adraga. There to meet them at the gates was Rebel, Mercy, Drizzle, Katrina and Storm. To his surprise Varick also saw Master Zi and Shahmaran waiting with them.

As they came within earshot Varick hailed Zi, "I did not expect you Zi, how is it you are here?"

"Let us go in Highness and I will update you on the current situation?", Zi smiled at Varick as he followed him through the gates with the others.

Varick instructed Rebel to take Raulf and Jonas to the palace dungeons and to make sure that a double guard was put in place. The rest entered the palace and made their way to their rooms to freshen up, Varick giving instructions to all to meet in the main hall for supper.

It was time for the evening meal when they all finally sat down in the main hall of the Palace. The huge table which was central in the room was laden with food and all tucked in heartily. Gentle music was playing in the background as the servants went around filling goblets with wine. Varick mopped up the last bit of gravy from his plate with some bread before addressing the room.

"Firstly, let me start by thanking Rebel for averting a disaster which could have meant the end of the games before they had even started", spoke Varick gravely. Rebel acknowledged with a slight bow. "At this point also, looking at Katrina I can see that your healing abilities are now in full force Rebel, I congratulate you on achieving something that we did not think was possible. The healing of another not of your own lineage. This is truly amazing and something we will need to explore further once the games are over". Katrina looked at Rebel, gratitude and admiration reflected in her eyes.

"Now let me focus on the games and how they will take place. We have three teams, Rebel with Storm, Raulf with Jonas, the third will be Zale and we believe his partner maybe his daughter Ara through bond-link. This is a good time Librarian Xin to fill everyone in on what you have discovered regarding what I asked of you", Varick looked at Xin indicating he should stand.

"Your Majesty", Xin stood up bowing to the King before he started to speak. Xin looked at Rebel, "My Prince you are truly exceptional and unique in that you are the first Dragongold to have been born on Earth. History has foretold of such a dragon but never has one been seen. So, there is very little information that I can give you regarding your powers and what you are capable of. You have already demonstrated, in a number of ways that you are quite different to the rest of the Dragonian Clan. In particular, your healing abilities they are truly exceptional. However, there has been one tale that has given me some cause for concern regarding a Dragongold", paused Xin.

"Well what is it man?", Tarrin muttered impatiently.

"Highness", Xin looked at Tarrin with a frown on his face, then continued.

"A golden sword made from Caysand with the markings of the five earthly elements is the only thing that can kill you", Xin looked at Varick to check if he should continue.

"Do we know if there is such a sword in existence Xin? questioned Rebel. "Not that I am aware off Highness" replied Xin.

"Please continue Librarian Xin". This time it was Zi who spoke.

"Raulf with his Blue Aura is also rare for a Dragonian. If a dragon is born with a blue aura, then one of two things can happen. They can either become one of the greatest magicians in the world, or the blue aura overpowers them and turns them towards evil ways, again their magic is still extremely powerful. However, I do believe that Rebel as a Dragongold can beat a dragon with a blue aura if ever they are in combat together. Unless of course, there does exist a sword made from Caysand as legend foretells.

“What about Zale and his daughter being bond-linked with him?”, Tarrin encouraged him to continue.

“Well that is an anomaly. Little has been written about being bond-linked with someone who has taken on the powers of another with whom they were bond-linked with. If you are a direct bond-linked, then the most powerful is the one who originated the link. The other is only the receiver, they cannot channel the power themselves. However, if you have gained your powers as I mentioned through losing the original bond then I could find nothing as to what happens to the power and how and if Zale has access to it”, Xin finished speaking and sat down.

“This may be a silly question but what is bond-linked and why is Zale involved in this?”, asked Rebel looking a little puzzled.

“Of course, Rebel you would not know what has happened since you were here. Manasa please could you repeat what you told us about the bonk-linked and the connection to Zale”. Manasa nodded and quickly relayed the information to those present again regarding Wyetta, Zale and their daughter Ara.

“Wait, so you’re saying that Wyetta was bond-linked to Ara and when she died her powers were passed onto Ara?”, Rebel repeated.

“Yessss, that is what I mean”, Manasa looked at Rebel as if to say, surely that’s what I just said.

“No”, Rebel said. “What do you mean NO?”, this again from Manasa.

"I mean that Wyetta is not dead so therefore they can't be bond-linked", Rebel looked at everyone in the room. "I'm sorry but I just couldn't get her out of my mind. That same night that I thought I had killed Wyetta, I had fallen asleep after my evening meal when she came to me in my dreams asking for my help. It was so real that I got up and went back out to where I had last seen her under the sea. When I found her, she was still breathing but only faintly", Rebel was interrupted by Zi.

"Where is she Rebel, you must tell us quickly? it is not safe to leave her on her own". The sense of urgency in Zi's voice struck a chord in everyone including Rebel.

"Master Zi I have imprisoned her in the dungeons under guard", Rebel jumped up as did the others. "Storm we will need you too", Zi instructed.

As Rebel, Zi and Storm made their way to the dungeons Varick looked at Manasa, "Queen Shahmaran, does this mean that Zale cannot bond-link and that Wyetta is still linked to her daughter?"

"Highness I cannot say. If Wyetta did actually 'die' for even a few secondsss, then I believe that the bond-link would have automatically shifted to her daughter. If that isss the case, then Wyetta is no longer a threat to usss. However, if she did not then she still has her powersss, which is not good for Zale. We will have to wait for Wyetta to be brought to usss. I think Katrina would be the best one to check this as she is most powerful in mind-linking", Manasa finished taking a sip of wine as she sat down.

"In your research did you find any information regarding this?". Varick directed the question to Xin. "No, Your Highness, I did not. I'm afraid this is another anomaly", Xin surmised. Varick nodded and frowned, "We will wait for them to get back then so that we can get answers to our questions. Katrina are you able to do what Manasa has suggested?"

Katrina nodded, "I am my Lord".

Storm, Zi and Rebel entered the dungeons with Rebel leading the way towards where Wyetta was being kept. As they made their way through the different passages, an ear-piercing scream echoed through the dungeons. Startled both Rebel and Storm broke into a run towards the direction of the scream.

As they approached the cell where Wyetta was being held, an unusual odour filled the air. Storm recognised it at once, it was the smell of burning flesh. They turned the corner and could see a body lying on the floor near Wyetta's cell. Wyetta herself was standing with her back to the wall furthest from the cell door. Two cells down, Raulf and Jonas were standing behind their cell door peering down to see what was happening.

Another guard was also on the floor, he looked alive, but he was also badly burned. Rebel went to him to see if he could help him. He laid his hands on the guards' chest and closed his eyes, blocking out the commotion around him. He started to mentally feel his way inside the body of the guard. As he did so Rebel could sense the pain the guard was in and he made his way to the area that had been badly burnt and started to heal from the inside out.

As Zi came around the corner, he saw Rebel leaning over

a body on the floor and the figure of a motionless guard on the floor still smoking slightly. He looked very dead. Quickly Zi muttered something under his breath, and he froze the moment. Only Rebel and Storm were still with him in time.

"Storm we need to question Wyetta first before we go to Raulf and Jonas. Only two people were capable of this, Raulf or Wyetta", said Zi as he moved to open the door to Wyetta's cell.

Zi snapped his fingers, Wyetta woke with a start, trying to back further but couldn't. Storm stood next to Zi, looking at Wyetta keenly for any reaction. "Wyetta, I am Master Zi, do you know where you are and who you are?" Zi asked.

"I am Wyetta, magician to the Thunder Dragons…", her voice petered off, the expression on her face looked puzzled. "I cannot feel my magic, what has happened to me?", she whispered.

"Did you kill the guard Wyetta?", Storm growled at Wyetta.

"She could not Storm, her magic has been lost. It seems that Manasa was right, Wyetta must have stopped breathing for a few seconds. It has now transferred to Ara her daughter", as Zi finished speaking Wyetta gave a low moan and slid to the floor holding her head in her hands.

"Then this has to be the work of Raulf", Storm leapt out of the cell to confront Raulf.

"Wait Storm", shouted Zi. "Let Rebel heal the guard so we can find out what happened. Then we can deal with the situation. In the meantime, please get me the Caysand Cloak from Prince Tarrin, as I believe he has brought his with him. I will wait here with Rebel until you return", instructed Zi as he knelt down near Rebel.

Storm returned a short time later with the cloak. Rebel was just getting up off the floor as he arrived, looking very drained. When Storm looked at the guard Rebel was helping, he was amazed. The burns had all but disappeared and he was starting to sit up slowly, groaning as he did so.

"Truly amazing Rebel", Storm commented as he handed Rebel some water. Storm had remembered that a desperate thirst was a consequence of the healing that Rebel performed, from when he had healed Katrina. He also handed some to the guard who by now was looking around dazed and confused.

"Guard, can you tell us what happened here?", asked Zi.

"All I can remember is that we were about to feed the prisoners when suddenly, a blue flame flashed across us and that is the last thing I remember, apart from the pain I felt when it hit me", the guard whispered slowly in-between taking huge gulps of water.

"So, it was Raulf!", exclaimed Rebel from where he was sat, water was dripping down his chin as he finished the pitcher Storm had brought.

"Storm come with me we will wrap Raulf with the cloak before I release him from the time lock", Zi instructed as he walked towards the cell where Raulf and Jonas were being kept.

Storm had picked up the keys for the prison cells which were lying on the floor next to the guard who had been killed. As he approached their cell, he could see that Jonas had his hands on the bars holding on tightly, this would make it difficult to open the cell door he thought to himself. Storm prised Jonas's fingers off one by one, before inserting the key and slowly opening the door as the two were still immediately behind it. Storm pushed at them slowly with the door and it wouldn't budge. Storm tried again with a slightly firmer push, this time it caused them both to topple backwards onto the floor. "Ooo… that's going to hurt", thought Storm to himself as he entered with Zi.

"Good Storm you have them in the correct position", Zi exclaimed with a slight smile on his face. "Please wrap them both up together in the Caysand Cloak".

As Storm finished rolling them both in the cloak, Zi uttered the words "Hold Fast", the cloak slowly moved, wrapping itself around the two even tighter. As it finished moving, Zi clicked his fingers.

Raulf moaned slowly as he felt pain in the back of his head. As he tried to move his hand up to where it hurt, he couldn't. He opened his eyes wider as realization dawned that once again, he had been trapped by the Caysand Cloak.

Raulf started to utter expletives, angrily Zi waived his hand across Raulf and uttered the word "Silence".

Raulf could move his mouth but no sound came out. After a few minutes of trying he gave up and just lay there.

"It seems that you are intent on getting yourself into further trouble Raulf. You go too far this time", Zi boomed out the last few words. "Storm leave them here as they are, we go back to the King". Zi left the cell and motioned for Storm, Rebel and the guard to follow. Storm glanced at Raulf before looking at Jonas shaking his head slowly. "You fool Jonas, you align yourself with someone who only thinks of himself, this will be your downfall", giving Jonas a disdainful look before walking out after Zi.

"What about Wyetta?". Rebel looked at Wyetta who was still sitting in the same position with her head held in her hands, weeping softly.

"Leave her as she is, she is harmless now, but may be very useful to us. Lock the cells guard and wait here", Zi instructed as he led the way down the passage and out of the dungeons.

They entered the hall where Varick and the rest were still waiting for their return.

CHAPTER NINETEEN

Ara looked towards her father who was standing in the same place he had stood every day since her mother had died.

Zale was at the edge of the entrance to his cave, looking out to sea. He missed Wyetta, it was only after she had been killed, did he realise how much he loved her…and now it was too late to tell her. He sighed deeply again.

“Father”, Ara whispered. “Father”, Ara repeated a little louder as Zale appeared to have not heard her.

“Yes Ara?”, responded Zale kneeling down, as she approached him, giving her a big hug.

“Father I wish to talk with you. Please may we go to Mother’s home, as I wish to speak to you there?” Ara looked at her father with her big eyes pleading for him to say yes.

“Why do we need to go there Ara? Surely, we can talk about this here”, Zale reasoned with her.

“No father, mother said if anything ever happened to her, I should take you there and show you something that she said could be very important to you in the future”, Ara finished hugging Zale even closer.

Wyetta lived nearly a days' flight away and Zale knew it would be cutting it fine for the Water Element Games if he went there now. However, he thought to himself, Wyetta would not have asked Ara to relay this to him if it wasn't important. Making the decision to go Zale turned to Ara, "Ara go get your warmest cloak and be ready to leave in one hour".

Zale went into his home and instructed the servants to prepare food for two days for both himself and Ara. He then made his way into his room to prepare for the long flight.

Wyetta had lived in the Wilderness Peaks, an area where the Caysand beaches finished and the mountainous region of the Peaks started. The mountains were many and stretched out as far as the eye could see. The high peaks were covered in snow and they looked very much like an army of dragons lining up for war. They were forbidding and dark, but Wyetta had loved them and had decided many years ago to move there to practice her powerful magic undisturbed by others.

Zale recalled back to when he had met her first. It was many years ago when the Thunder Dragons were celebrating the day of the Thunder Moon. It was the most important day of the year for the Thunder Dragons.

In the seventh month of every year it was the time of the Thunder Moon, it was an auspicious time as it meant that all the Thunder Dragons had an opportunity to find a mate plus it would also be the start of the wet season.

The Thunder Dragons lived for the wet season as light shows in the sky were a daily occurrence and the different sounds of thunder that accompanied them felt as though the gods were singing to them.

The annual gathering always took place on the Caysand Beach. The weather always tended to be warm this time of year and Zale as Leader of the Thunder Dragons was sitting at a table with some of his friends when he looked out towards the sea. Zale could feel his stomach tighten as he recalled his reaction when he saw Wyetta for the first time. She was walking along the water's edge, her long dark hair flowing behind her. Wyetta wore a shimmering ivory coloured dress which had shaped her body as the breeze blew in from the sea. She had looked stunningly beautiful and Zale knew she was the one for him.

Zale broke out of his reverie as he heard Ara's small footsteps coming in his direction. He quickly fastened his cloak around him and made his way out of his room to meet her.

Zale had fashioned a small rope seat out of Caysand which fixed onto his back for Ara to sit in, as she was still too young to transform herself fully into her dragon.

Also, the long journey would have been too much for her to complete on her own anyway.

Ara was in that seat now and the magic of the Caysand held her fast as Zale flew high into the sky. They had left early in the day and Zale hoped to be at the Wilderness Peaks by nightfall. They would spend the night there before making the arduous journey back.

They were lucky, the sky was a bright blue with the sun hot on their backs it was going to be a good journey. A swift breeze was blowing which also boosted Zale's speed, as it caught beneath his wings, giving him a much-needed lift making it less tiring as he flew.

The journey had been uneventful, as they got closer, Zale could see the mountain peaks in the distance. Wyetta's home was on the second highest peak in the region and only became visible as you got closer to it. It was slightly hidden behind a huge jutting rock so Zale had to swing out wide before he could land on its platform. Zale had been here many times in the past and knew it well.

He helped Ara out of the rope seat before he transformed back to his human self. Both entered the cave hesitantly, acutely aware that the last time they had come here, Wyetta was waiting to greet them.

A small sob escaped from Ara as they entered the cave, Zale stooped down and scooped her up into his arms, "Hush daughter, all will be well. Let us go to the main chamber, we can discuss what it is your mother wanted you to tell me there", spoke Zale comfortingly.

Wyetta's presence was everywhere causing unbelievable pain. They entered the large chamber which was very dark and cold. Zale placed Ara onto one of the many scattered cushions in the room before going round and lighting the various candles Wyetta always lit. Once done he sat down next to Ara holding her hand, he encouraged her to speak.

"Okay Ara what is it you needed to tell me?" he asked gently.

"I have to show you father", Ara spoke softly getting down off his lap she made her way to a tapestry hung on the wall. She pulled it aside slowly and to Zale's surprise, a small hidden door made of wood was revealed. Ara whispered something under her breath causing the door to swing open into the room. Ara entered a narrow dark passage, as she did so she looked back at her father and encouraged him to follow her.

"Where does this go Ara?", questioned Zale.

"Follow me father I will show you", Ara's voice echoed in the passageway as she walked further into the darkness. Neither Zale nor Ara were concerned about the darkness, as dragons they really had no need of light as they turned on their night vision to see perfectly well.

The passage wound its way downwards for a while until Ara stopped at another wooden door. Again, she muttered something under her breath and like the previous door this one also swung open. This time however, a small cave was revealed. As they entered, the cave appeared completely empty.

"Ara there is nothing here!", exclaimed Zale, "What is it you expected to be here?", uttered Zale a little frustrated.

"Wait father, watch", instructed Ara. Ara stood to one side of the room indicating to Zale to stand next to her. Ara sidestepped two steps away from him, before she raised her arms into the air. With her hands she started to make intricate movements, as they weaved in and out through the air, she began to raise both her arms above her head with fingertips outstretched. Holding that position for a few seconds, she suddenly brought both arms down with her fingers now pointing to the middle of the room.

To Zale's amazement sparks started to fly mid-air, increasing rapidly until suddenly they stopped leaving behind a plume of smoke. Zale was utterly fascinated by the display and at first did not register what was in front of him.

As the smoke dispersed Zale could see a golden sword standing rigid in the centre of the room, with the tip of the sword touching the floor. Etched along the whole length of the sword were the five earthly elements. Zale gasped as he recognised what it was.

Ara stood where she was as she watched her father walk towards the sword.

"It was created by mother for you father. She said she had a vision many years ago of the birth of a Dragongold. She told me if anything ever happened to her, I must bring you here no matter what", Ara stopped speaking and just stood there watching her father.

Zale had not touched the sword yet, he just walked around it, taking in its magnificence. It was the most beautiful sword he had ever seen, and he had seen many in his lifetime. He lifted his hand towards the hilt of the sword and touched it reverently. Slowly he curled his fingers around the hilt until he had a firm grasp before lifting it off the floor.

As soon as he moved the sword an electric current ran up his arm and into his body. Shocked Zale immediately knew that the sword had bonded with him, it belonged to him, it was now a part of him, he could command it any time. He did not know how he knew all about the sword, he just did.

The sword spoke to him instructing him what to do, it was teaching him how to master it, Zale thought to himself totally bewildered.

Obeying Zale gave the first instruction, "Vanish", Zale whispered the word, the sword then disappeared into thin air. He held his hand up amazed, "Attack", the sword reappeared just as quickly in his hand.

He turned and looked at Ara, her little face was a picture. "Thank you, Ara, this is most amazing".

"It was mother, she is the one who made it for you, she loved you very much", Ara whispered quietly.

"Yes, I miss her too Ara. We must get ready to leave at dawn if I am to get back in time for the start of the Water Element Games Ara. Let us eat before we sleep. Lead the way out again my dear".

CHAPTER TWENTY

Varick was in the middle of finalising the details of the Water Element challenge with Librarian Xin, when Manasa entered the room.

"Majesty", uttered Manasa, at the same time she gave Xin a look which told him he needed to make himself scarce. Varick also saw the look and nodded to Xin who had turned to him for permission to leave.

"Manasa, what can I do for you?", responded Varick.

"I come to inform you of what has been arranged for the Water Element Games as per your request King Varick. Again however, I would remind you, that no matter what, Raulf will be mine at the end of the Five Element Challengesss", Manasa finished with a long hiss on the last word.

"I have not forgotten Manasa. Please tell me what you have arranged", Varick spoke quietly, sadness tinged his words.

"I have arranged for the Pelamis Yellow Bellies to aid Rebel in the games", Manasa was in the middle of speaking, when they heard the words, "No they will not". Both looked around to see who had uttered the words.

"Who goes there? Reveal yourself", Varick commanded.

“It is I Uncle, can you not see me?” chuckled Rebel

“I recognise your voice Rebel, where are you?”, Varick was irritated; Rebel could tell by the way he spoke.

Rebel pulled open the Caysand cloak to reveal himself sitting at the same table as Varick and Manasa.

“Rebel how long have you been here like that?”, blustered Varick.

“I followed Manasa and slipped in as Librarian Xin left. I was testing the cloak to see how good it was. It seems that I came just in time. Why have you arranged for the Pelamis to assist in the games Uncle?, Surely that is cheating!” exclaimed Rebel.

“He is right brother, it is cheating”, Tarrin revealed himself as he was also wrapped in his own Caysand Cloak and was sitting next to Rebel.

“It seems you need to get your family in order Your Majesty, please let me know if you still require the help of the Serpentes”, Manasa lisped disapprovingly peering at Rebel, then Tarrin before leaving the room.

“Varick why would you do this? Do you not think Rebel can win?”, Tarrin asked Varick softly.

“I know you have doubts brother worrying about both Raulf and Rebel. But we must remain resolute and follow the rules of the Games to the letter. Otherwise we may lose the Kingdom anyway if the Gods find that we have cheated”, finished Tarrin.

Varick closed his eyes and nodded, "You are right brother, we must remain resolute. I have spoken to Librarian Xin who has informed me that the Water Element Games will be held tomorrow at Noon".

"Uncle what will be the Water Element Challenge?", questioned Rebel.

Varick looked at his nephew, "It will be the Riva Gauntlet".

Rebel noticed that his father had visibly paled as he heard the words. "Father, are you okay? What is the Riva Gauntlet?"

Tarrin looked at Varick, "Why brother, why the Riva Gauntlet? Surely you could have chosen a different challenge?"

"I have no choice in the matter this time brother. The challenges for the Dragon Games' were always decided by the Gods, it is they who have chosen the Riva Gauntlet", Varick looked as disturbed as Tarrin as he spoke.
"Please can someone tell me what the Riva Gauntlet is?", Rebel again asked looking at both his father and his uncle.

"It is the most difficult of the Water Element Challenges and involves the challenger to swim through the Riva Gauntlet which starts at the seashore and continues for ten leagues across the sea", Tarrin explained, "However, the challenge is swum under the water and you are only allowed to come up for air during the challenge. The God of the Sea will create many challenges for you with the water which will slow you down, hurt you or even kill you". As Tarrin finished speaking he put both his hands on Rebels' shoulders, "Son it is most difficult for the Ledary Dragons as we are land dragons. This is the reason why Thunder Dragons inevitably win this particular challenge as they have the ability to hold their breath under the water for long periods of time".

"Do not worry father, I am not concerned for myself in this challenge. I know that Storm as a Felinia Black will not like this challenge. It is with Storm that I must discuss how we will complete this. Uncle I will take my leave and speak with Storm", Rebel stood up to leave, but before he did, he handed back the Caysand Cloak he was wearing to Varick. "Your Cloak uncle, I have discovered many of its secrets, and if I may I would like to use it for the Fire Element Challenge when that takes place", Varick nodded his agreement as Rebel left.

"Brother did you reconsider the 'Judgement?' Tarrin asked of his brother.

"Given that the Gods have chosen the Riva Gauntlet for the Water Element Challenge, I suspect they will be just as harsh with the other four challenges. I think because of this, I would agree with you that it will be too much to also allow a 'Judgement'. So no, I will not be requesting a 'Judgement' from the Gods, finished Varick.

Tarrin gave a huge sigh of relief, "Let us go and find Lexi and Althea so we may inform them of the Challenge and check that the preparations are in order".

Ara fell instantly asleep as her head touched her pillow back at Adraga. They had arrived late from the Wilderness

Peaks as the weather was against them on the way back. After a quick meal Zale had suggested that Ara get to bed, to which she readily agreed.

Standing in the middle of his room, Zale stretched his right arm out in front of him, whispering the word, "Attack". The sword appeared immediately in his hand. Turning it slowly, he absorbed the intricate details of the etchings on the blade. "Wyetta had created a masterpiece", he thought to himself, silently applauding her. Zale stood there for a long while making himself familiar with all that the sword could do. The etchings meant something, he knew this, they had a purpose he needed to know everything that the sword was capable of, before the challenges started.

Zale and Ara had been met by one of his guards when they had arrived back from the Peaks. The guard had handed him a note from King Varick, informing Zale that the Water Element Challenge would be the Riva Gauntlet. Zale had heard of this challenge; he also knew it was the most difficult of all.

He looked again at the etchings on the sword, focusing on the Water Element etching, he slowly touched the engraving. As he did so the engraving started to change, turning aqua blue, rippling outwards across the blade towards the hilt. To Zale's amazement, the whole sword had changed to water, becoming translucent.

Zale swung the sword to slice an object on a table close to where he was standing, to his amazement, the sword cut straight through it only leaving behind a small puddle of water. Testing it further, he touched the tip of the sword to the edge of a cup that was also on the table, water flowed into the cup filling it to the brim.

Deciding he wanted to know what would happen if he touched the engraving of Fire, he slowly brushed the tips of his fingers over the etching for the Fire Element. The image of the flame started to glow red before suddenly bursting into flame. Zale's automatic reaction was to release the sword from his hand as he felt the heat. Even though he had opened his hand the sword remained in place with flames licking outwards from the blade. Realization dawned on Zale that the hilt only felt warm in his hand, waiving the sword to and fro he watched the flames dancing and flickering in the darkness of his room. Eventually he stopped and uttered the word "Vanish".

Zale lay down on his bed, his mind full of the challenges of the Riva Gauntlet taking place the following day and his two opponents. He had already named his partner to King Varick in a note he had sent two days ago. Ara, who had bond-linked with him when they were in the Wilderness Peaks, was going to be his partner. That bond-link had given him a world of knowledge and his mind was full of all that was Wyetta's magic.

"Father do not worry about the magic, I will help you with that", startled at hearing Ara's voice in his head, Zale sat up quickly.

"Ara how are you doing this?", Zale asked crossly.

"Father we are now bond-linked we can both listen and hear each other at any time", Zale could hear the smile in her voice as she spoke. Zale hesitated before he spoke again, "Ara I am going to block you from my mind and will only allow you access as and when required for the games. Now go to sleep".

"Yes Father", responded Ara in a small voice.

Somehow the process of how to block someone from entering one's mind had popped into his head as he spoke to Ara and with a quick thought, he blocked her. Sighing deeply, he again lay back on his bed closing his eyes, it was going to be a long night he thought to himself, with a million thoughts racing through his head in anticipation of the Games the following day.

CHAPTER TWENTY-ONE

A billowing white Dias had been erected at the point where the cliffs finished and the Caysand beach started, affording it some shelter from the warm salty air blowing in from the sea. King Varick along with his brother Prince Tarrin and their wives Queen Althea and Princess Lexi were all sat on four small thrones which had been placed on the Dias. They had arrived early so they could portray a united front to the various families of the Kingdom who had arrived for the Games.

Varick had hoped that by doing this, it would dispel any potential troublemakers, from even starting to think about causing any issues.

As Rebel and Storm were taking part in the games, it had been decided that Prince Jai, Princess Sophia with her fiancé High Lord Sylvest, Katrina, Dribble, Crick, Mercy, and Keon would mingle amongst the crowds to ensure that they could talk down any who may be stirring trouble. Beda remained with the Queen as leader of the Warrior Maids, along with Conall, Master of the Kings Guard and a small contingency of their guards.

Conall and Beda looked at each other and nodded, both acknowledging the importance of the day and the role that they, with their respective units would play. They had discussed long into the night the plans for the security of the games. As they both looked around the vast expanse of the beach, they could see dotted around the colourful uniform of both their units. Beda could also occasionally see one of Rebel's team mingling among the crowd.

The twelve families had all come with a full entourage, some having arrived in their human form and others in their animal. If the games did not have to be played to the death, it would have been a wonderful day thought Beda to herself. Sighing inwardly, thinking back to the night when this had all started, she could not believe that nearly three full moons had passed since that fateful night. This night would be the time of the Thunder Moon and the beginning of the wet season, which favoured the Thunder Dragons.

Beda glanced towards the sea, the waves gently lapping against the shore, the water looked calm as far as the eye could see. No one had witnessed the Dragon Games in their lifetime, the unknown was creating an unusual feeling inside her and many others no doubt. The arrival of the contestants would signal the start of the Water Element Game. Looking back at King Varick and the rest of the Royal Family, she could sense that they too were nervous of what was to come. Turning to face the sea, her eyes locked with Conall, whose concerned expression mirrored hers. Both gave a silent acknowledgement to each other before resuming watch.

Rebel sat facing Storm at a table by the window in his room, "I do not know what will be involved in the Riva Gauntlet Storm, do you have any ideas what it may entail?"

"What I do know is that it has been the cause of many deaths in the past. The Gods have control, and they ensure that each Gauntlet is different from the last. It was the Steaming Sea that caused the deaths of two of the participants in the very last Dragon Games", Storm paused looking at Rebel.

"As Felinia both Jonas and I will be disadvantaged in the Gauntlet. Of all the Elements, Water is the one we hate most", Storm finished.

"I was aware of this Storm, what is it that I can do during the Gauntlet that can aid you?" questioned Rebel.

"Do not leave me behind, no matter what happens you must make sure that I am with you at all times during the Gauntlet. To be separated will weaken us both, but for me it would mean my death!", Storm looked at Rebel sombrely before standing up and indicating to Rebel that he should do the same.

Rebel clasped Storm's arm in a gesture of friendship, "I will do all in my power to ensure that we are together throughout Storm. I will not lose you".

When they arrived at the King's Dias, they could see Zale approaching with his young daughter Ara holding his hand. Nodding in acknowledgement they all knelt in front of King Varick. Rebel noted that Prince Raulf had arrived before them and was being held under guard along with Jonas on the far side of the Dias.

Instructing them all to stand, Varick turned towards Master Zi who had just arrived, "Master Zi, I believe you will be overseeing the Gauntlet, is that right?"

"It is Highness", Zi responded before addressing the three contestants. "As you can see, three platforms have been erected by the edge of the sea. You will all start from these platforms, the end of the Gauntlet is marked with a Red marker, the first to return back onto the platform will win the Gauntlet", Zi indicated by waiving his arm towards the platforms.

"I remind you all that this Gauntlet has been devised by the Gods, which may and can result in death. Please make your way to your platforms for the start of the Riva Gauntlet", Zi announced loudly. A signal was given to the drummers close by, who began to beat their drums rhythmically, announcing to all the start of the Games.

The emblem for each of the contestants had been erected in front of the platforms, with Prince Raulf having the middle platform, Rebel was to his left facing the sea and Zale to his right.

Zale had a chair placed on the platform for Ara, "Ara dear you will sit here. We will communicate via bond-link", stated Zale in a voice that brooked no argument.

Raulf indicated to Jonas to jump into a small rope cage he had had constructed, that was strapped onto his back. "You want me to transform!", exclaimed Jonas looking scared. "I cannot do this in my animal form, it will kill me".

"You will transform, as I am not prepared to carry you as a human, it will slow us down", responded Raulf intimidatingly, flaring his blue aura as he did so. Jonas jumped out of reach quickly giving Raulf a desperate angry look.

Defeated, Jonas transformed into his animal. Jonas was a Catom, his ears were notched in various places, scratches were also visible on his nose. He was extremely unkempt and Raulf looked at him with disdain. Jonas miaowed loudly in protest before jumping into the basket. Raulf sealed the gap tying it tight with a leather strap.

Rebel on the other hand had arranged for a leather saddle to be strapped to his back, with a harness for Storm to hold him in place. Transforming to his dragon, Rebel indicated to Storm to climb aboard.

With all three pairs of contestants ready, Zi signalled to the drummers to stop beating their drums. Apart from the sound of the sea and the waves lapping on the shore there was complete silence, as all waited to see what would happen next.

Five minutes had passed with nothing happening, the crowd becoming restless had started to jeer and shout at no one in particular. When suddenly, someone in the crowd shouted "LOOK!", pointing towards the sea.

Rebel looked in the direction the man was pointing and gasped. A white foam was rolling towards them, reaching nearly fifty feet high and a league across. The closer it came the more ominous it looked.

"Be ready Storm, we shall leave as soon as Zi gives the signal", shouted Rebel as the noise from the crowd was getting louder the closer the foam got to the shore.

Zi held up both his hands in readiness to give the signal... "Be ready, be safe!", he shouted and brought both his hands down together signalling the start of the challenge. The crowds roared in anticipation, cheering for their favourite.

The first to take flight was Zale who had leapt into the sky as soon as Zi had started to move his arms downwards. Some in the crowd shouted at him in annoyance for starting before Zi had finished the signal, but to no avail. The Riva Gauntlet had started.

Rebel and Storm were completely enveloped by the white foam. Unable to see anything, Rebel closed his eyes. He heard Storm moaning from behind, "Storm is all okay with you?".

"Rebel the foam is burning my skin, is there anything you can do?", Storm leant forward to whisper into Rebel's ear. In response, Rebel flared his aura creating a vacuum of six inches around them. "Thank you Rebel", whispered Storm in response.

"I can guide you through this Rebel using my cat senses". Storm used his knees to indicate to Rebel which way to move. They flew like this for what seemed like an eternity, when suddenly, the foam just disappeared. Rebel could see Zale and Raulf just slightly ahead of him. To his horror he could also see a rogue wave heading towards them. They had no time to fly over it as it crashed straight into them causing Rebel to lose his balance, he tumbled over himself, rolling backwards and downwards for what seemed an age.

As the wave hit him, he heard rather than saw Raulf and Zale roar loudly as they were simultaneously hit by the wave. Rebel struggled to regain his balance and found himself bumping along the sea floor being pushed backwards and then forwards with the strong movements of the wave. Grimacing in pain as the coral ripped at his body, Rebel was also conscious of Storm who was strapped to his back, Rebel again flared his aura to protect Storm. As he managed to regain some form of balance, he could see Raulf's blue aura just ahead of him, the blue light was moving quickly towards the surface.

Of Zale there was no sign. Signalling to Storm to hold on, Rebel folded his wings tightly against his body and waived his tail side to side quickly to push them towards the surface. Gasping for air, Storm squeezed his knees tightly into Rebel's sides indicating that he was in trouble.

Recognising the signal, Rebel thrashed his tail faster, pulling his legs in closer to his body to become more streamlined. As he reached the surface, he flicked his tail hard clearing the water and immediately opened his wings to take flight. Rebel could hear Storm coughing and spluttering behind him. Relieved Rebel swooped back down and landed on the water so both he and Storm could catch their breath.

Zale had been just as shocked by the rogue wave as the others, however, having encountered them many times before as a Thunder Dragon, he knew exactly what to do. As it approached, he quickly tucked his wings to his side and stretched himself out in a straight line. As he entered the wave, he flicked his flattened tail, a trademark of the Thunder Dragons, up and down causing him to move through the wave rapidly. Positioning his body to head downwards, he moved quickly until he was below the wave and under the sea. Zale continued to swim underwater until he had passed the body of the wave, eventually coming up on the other side to calmer waters.

Giving a quick look around to see if the other two were near he gave a quick whoop as he saw neither.

He leapt up into the air and started to wing his way over the sea, when suddenly, he felt a whoosh of air which pushed him forcibly back down into the water. Shocked Zale looked up towards the sky and to his utter amazement the sky had parted to reveal the Gods watching the Gauntlet.

So unexpected was this that Zale had stopped moving, submerging under the water he came up spluttering seawater. A voice entered his head, "Zale of the Thunder Dragons, you cannot fly from this point onwards in the Gauntlet, do not try it again or you will be eliminated, permanently".

Zale looked up, but this time could see nothing, the sky had closed, but the warning remained. Looking around him as he bobbed in the water, still shocked at what had happened, he saw a blue light coming towards him from a distance. Realising it was Raulf, he quickly took a deep breath and submerged further into the water, flicking his tail swimming away quickly from the blue light.

Raulf reached the surface of the water and gasped loudly as he took in a huge gulp of air. His blue aura had faded as he lay limply in the water. He had not expected the rogue wave, giving him no chance to take a breath before he was submerged.

It was only when he heard Jonas mewling quietly that he realised he was still strapped on his back in the basket. "You still alive", Raulf sneered, before looking back at the wave which by now had calmed enough, for him to be able to see the crowds on the beach. Giving a quick backward glance, Raulf started to move in the direction of the red marker which was still quite far away.

As he moved, Rebel flew out of the water near him, with a quick flap of his wings, Rebel cleared the water before landing back on the surface.

Raulf could see Storm holding on tightly, blood was pouring from his back colouring the sea red around them. He also noticed that Rebel had huge gashes across his body which were also bleeding. A smile spread across his face as he realised that the two were weakened by their injuries. Raulf quickly dived under the water and swam away towards the red marker.

Storm flinched as something slid against him, flinching again, when it nudged him on the back. “Rebel we are surrounded by the Pelamis”, Storm spoke quietly so as not to attract the attention of the snakes. Rebel could see the Pelamis writhing in the water around them, hundreds of them curling up and over themselves, their dark grey bodies barely visible from above. It was only when their yellow underbellies were revealed did you realise, they were there.

It was the scent of blood that had attracted them to Storm and Rebel. Rebel knew that their venom was toxic and could kill. “Storm do not move. I will try to heal us as well as move us slowly out of their midst. Put your hands on my shoulders Storm, I shall heal you first”, whispered Rebel as he started to move ever so slowly through the knot of snakes.

Rebel let out a small roar as he felt the bites of numerous snakes attach themselves to his tail as he started to move it slowly side to side. Storm felt Rebels’ pain through the healing, and almost immediately felt Rebel weaken. Lifting his hands of Rebel’s shoulders, he quickly whispered to Rebel,

"Heal yourself first, I can feel the venom weaken you. If you die, we both die", instructed Storm.

Rebel reared his head in acknowledgement turning the healing inwards to himself, something he had never performed before. He marvelled at what he could 'see' as he travelled within his body, removing the venom from his veins before starting to heal the large gashes on his body. The Pelamis recoiled as their teeth were forcibly pushed out by Rebels magic. Storm could see a gap forming between Rebel and the snakes, as those who had been touched by the magic silently warned the others not to bite the Dragongold. Before long, the last of the Pelamis disappeared into the dark murky waters leaving behind the bodies of those who had been touched by Rebels magic.

Storm was weakened and close to losing unconsciousness when Rebel urgently nudged him awake, instructing him to again put his hands on his shoulders. Rebel realised as he was healing Storm that he had nearly lost him, so weakened had he become by the loss of blood and the venom of the Pelamis. Rebel sighed with relief as he could feel Storm becoming stronger with the healing, bringing him back from the cusp of death.

Zale moved quickly through the water marvelling at how easy it had been to get this far. "Ara? Can you hear me? Zale tried to make contact via bond-link, closing his eyes as he did so. "Yes father, I can. Where are you father? We cannot see any of you", responded Ara with a slight waver in her voice.

"Ara I am ahead of everyone, it seems as though I might...", Zale stopped speaking suddenly, as his face smashed into something hard and cold. Shocked, Zale roared with pain recoiling backwards, turning around in the water to regain his balance. He turned to see what he had hit, stopping himself quickly from moving any further, staying motionless, shocked at what he was looking at.

He was surrounded by brinicles, hundreds of them as far as he could see. He had heard of them but never encountered them before. Zale stared mesmerized as he watched new ones forming in front of him, not daring to move as he recalled that if you got caught in one as it was forming you could easily get killed. They were beautiful to look at, reminding him of the air funnels that formed on land, only these were of ice and formed underwater.

"Father, father, are you okay?", Ara was literally shouting at him in his mind. "Yes, yes Ara, I cannot talk right now, I am surrounded by brinicles, some which are still forming around me. I must concentrate if I am to get out of here alive", Zale responded. "Is there any magic that might help me that you can think off Ara?".

"Shielding magic father, I think that will help you get through", as soon as Ara had said the words, Zale knew what he had to do to shield himself.

He quickly transformed to his human self, before shielding, this made him much smaller than his dragon, making it easier for him to navigate the brinicles.

"Thank you Ara, I will be in touch again once I get past this", Zale realised that the shielding also allowed him to breathe normally as he moved slowly through the ice twisters without having to go up to the surface for air.

Zale heard a muffled roar echo in the distance, not waiting or looking to see who it was, he continued on his way to the red marker and the finish line, hoping that he did not come across anything else before then.

Raulf dived under after watching the Pelamis surround Rebel and Storm. So occupied was he with them that he dived head first under the water and immediately became caught in the formation of a brinicle. He screamed loudly at the pain, as the tip of his wing became trapped within the ice. Raulf could see that his wing had started to discolour and freeze. The discolouration was travelling slowly up his wing causing Raulf to panic, flaring his blue aura with the hope that it would release his wing. It did not!

"Jonas, Jonas, can you hear me?", strangled out Raulf as the pain was becoming unbearable. "I need to break the hold of the brinicle, any suggestions?"

"You have to kill me Raulf, I can help you when I am dead, but don't extinguish me", Jonas screeched out.

"What are you saying Jonas? How can you help if you are dead!", Raulf roared frustratedly at Jonas. "Raulf, JUST DO IT", shouted Jonas. In pain and panicking Raulf did as he was instructed, flaring his blue aura. Jonas let out a long squeal before finally succumbing to death.

"Jonas? Jonas? Where are you?... Raulf spoke urgently.

"I am releasing you, look towards your wing", Jonas was floating near the brinicle. "How did you do that?", Raulf gasped as he saw him. "Do not panic Prince Raulf, I am a spirit in my human form. Remember, I have nine lives and I have just used one up. You owe me a life!", with that Jonas started to make a high-pitched noise which became louder and louder. Raulf covered his ears as they started to throb, the pain was unbearable. Suddenly, the brinicle and many around it, shattered into thousands of shards, leaving Raulf floating in a sea full of mini icicles.

With his wing freed, Raulf made his way to the surface, taking a deep breath as he broke out into the fresh air. To his amazement, swimming towards him was Jonas, back in his cat form.

"You did well Jonas, now climb back into the basket and let us continue with the race", spoke Raulf, still grimacing at the pain from his injured wing.

Jonas swam up to Raulf and started to climb up his back, entering the basket quickly. This time however, Raulf did not tie the opening, leaving it open for Jonas to climb in and out.

Submerging slowly, Raulf warily looked around at the brinicles deciding to swim to the bottom of the sea where the narrow part of the brinicles touched the seabed. From there he slowly swam through the icicles wending his way forward cautiously.

Rebel turned to Storm, "Are you ready to continue?"

"Yes Rebel, let us go we are losing time", Storm patted Rebel on the back as he spoke, "and thank you for saving my life".

Rebel flared his aura before he submerged slowly, wary that the Pelamis may still be lurking under the water. As he submerged, he slowed and stopped looking at the ethereal scene in front of him. He heard Storm exclaim loudly at what they were looking at. The brinicles glistened in the sunlight filtering through from above, known as the "fingers of death", long icicles funnelled towards the seabed creating a forest of ice tentacles.

Rebel made his way slowly back towards the surface, turning towards Storm as he cleared the water. "Any suggestions Storm?"

"Can you recall your training in the Valley of the Five Rebel? On our way back to the Kingdom you toyed with a stream making the water do as you willed it. Can you manipulate the water now to create a tunnel that can see us safely across the brinicles?"

Rebel transformed to human, with Storm still strapped on his back, turning around to look at him, he grinned, "I knew there was a reason I brought you along".

"Hold on tightly Storm this is going to be fun!", shouted Rebel as he waived his hands in a circular motion within the water. The water rose up rotating quickly anticlockwise, creating a funnel as far as the eye could see. Fish caught up in the funnel, jumped and danced in and out of the water creating a colourful display. "Be ready Storm we are going to fly through the funnel as fast as we can, I do not know how long I can hold it for", shouted Rebel above the noise.

Storm nodded in agreement as Rebel transformed back to Dragon. Rebel looked up at the sky and could see the Gods watching him in amusement. Zi was also watching, a big smile on his face as he turned towards Yinshi of the Panthera who was frowning darkly, "Technically, Yinshi he is not flying in the air but through the sea in the funnel, so he is within the rules", spoke Zi matter of factly, secretly applauding Rebel at his ingenuity.

Rebel gave a quick cheeky salute to the Gods, before leaping into the funnel of water with a huge flap of his wings. Storm clung on tightly to Rebel, as the water was rushing around them noisily, drenching them both as they made their way through.

They were both exhausted as they approached the end of the funnel, Rebel with a final burst of energy flew quickly towards the exit. They finally cleared the water funnel into the open air, before landing back on the surface of the sea. Transforming back into his human form, Rebel released Storm from his back before floating, facing upwards to look at the blue sky.

As they both lay there floating silently and catching their breath, they heard a small splashing sound coming from a short-distance away. Both quickly lifted their heads and turned in the direction of the noise. It was Zale, now in his human form you could see blood dripping from an injury to his mouth, which he was trying to clean before he attracted any unwelcome visitors.

It was only when he had finished splashing the water over his face that he realised Rebel and Storm were watching him. Giving them a quick nod, he turned and started to swim, heading towards the finish line.

As Rebel and Storm started to do the same, Raulf emerged in front of them with Jonas still strapped in the cage on his back. Raulf sneered at them, instructing Jonas to get out of the cage and transform quickly back to human. "Swim Jonas, we must get ahead of them all if we are to win the race", Raulf shouted urgently at Jonas as both Rebel and Storm swam past them at an unusually fast pace.

Zale panicked as he realised what he was caught up in, unaware until the last moment of the danger of the maelstrom. Trapped in the strong pull of the water, Zale could not free himself as it turned in a huge circular motion. He had never seen one so big, or so strong, he could see many creatures of the sea both big and small caught up in it as he moved downwards in the huge liquid spiral.

"Ara, I need your help", Zale urgently shouted to his daughter via mind-meld.

"Father, what is it?", Ara responded almost immediately.

"I am trapped within a maelstrom Ara I need to use your magical energy as well as mine to be able to free myself from it. Let me tap into it now", Zale was tiring fast as he tried to keep his head above the water as he rotated round and round.

Ara opened her mind and Zale jumped in, drawing on her energy. As it flowed through his body, he felt himself become stronger with the extra magical power. Zale continued to move in the direction of the flow until he felt strong enough to do what he must to free himself.

Suddenly, he saw Rebel and Storm swirl past him quickly, both also caught up in the maelstrom, although he noticed that Storm was attached to Rebel with a long cord. Moments later, Raulf and then Jonas could be seen further ahead and above him as they too were caught. It was clear that Jonas was struggling as he was on his own, and as a Felinia he could not cope, not even in his human form.

Jonas was transforming back and forth, unwittingly to his cat and then his human form, unable to stop it as he drowned and died many times within the maelstrom.

Rebel too had noticed Jonas' predicament, "Storm we have to help him!", Rebel shouted above the sound of the water.

"If we do that Rebel, we will lose the challenge. But I agree with you, we cannot let him die like this", Storm responded.

"I am going to try to slow us down, so he is near us as he turns in the water, we can then 'catch' him. Help me in this Storm, make yourself bigger to resist the flow and swim against it", instructed Rebel.

Zale looked up and saw what Rebel and Storm had done, making an instant decision to do the same he turned to get himself ready in case they failed.

Raulf was ahead of Jonas by nearly two hundred feet, when he swirled past Rebel and Storm. He could not believe what they were doing, "Why would he do this for a Felinia? He would lose the race", he thought to himself as he moved quickly in the water, Raulf geared himself up to pull out of the maelstrom using all his strength, waiting for the right moment to then fly upwards and outwards.

As he reached Zale, who had also turned against the flow, he sneered at him shouting, "YOU HAVE ALL LOST, I WILL BE KING", laughing wildly as he sped up quickly before suddenly ejecting himself out into the middle of the maelstrom where it was free of water and opened his wings.

Catching the air under his wings he flapped wildly upwards to the opening of the maelstrom.

"Storm, Jonas approaches be ready to catch him", shouted Rebel. Rebel could see that Jonas was currently in his human form, "so should be easy to get hold of", he thought to himself. Just as Jonas was close enough for Rebel to grab hold, he transformed back to cat. So quickly did he transform that Rebel lost him, shouting quickly to Storm, "Catch him Storm".

Storm went to grab him, but too late as Jonas in his cat form was moving much faster as his body was smaller.

Storm looked at Jonas in despair as he travelled further away from him in the swirling water. "Look Storm, it seems Zale is also going to try and catch him", Rebel indicating with his head in the direction of where Zale was. They watched keenly as they allowed themselves once more to be caught in the swirl of the water, to see if Zale could do, what they could not, save Jonas.

Jonas was fast approaching Zale, who readied himself to catch him. As Jonas approached, he had turned back to human and Zale could see no movement from him. Zale went to grab his arm, but missed, he then quickly went to grab his leg, managing to catch him by the ankle. The flow of the water was dragging hard at Jonas trying to pull him out of Zale's grasp.

When suddenly, Jonas transformed back to cat, his paw so small slipped out of Zale's hand and Jonas was lost. Jonas' body remained in his cat form as it moved quickly in the flow of the water, until it was out of sight.

“Zale”, shouted Rebel, “Pull yourself out now, otherwise it will be too late you are reaching the bottom of the maelstrom and you will be lost”.

Rebel was back as his dragon, with Storm sitting on his back as he hovered in the air near Zale. “Do it now quickly Zale, jump onto my back, I will fly us all out”, Rebel flew closer to Zale following him as he turned in the water.

Zale looked down and saw that what Rebel said was true, he had little time. Gathering speed in the water, Zale transformed and gave a mighty flick of his tail pushing himself out of the water. Opening his wings quickly, he turned to Rebel, “Move Rebel, I can look after myself”. Zale gave a backward glance at Rebel before making his way out with huge flaps of his wings.

Rebel followed suit, glad that Zale had managed to free himself, he moved quickly upwards clearing the maelstrom, he flew over the sea for a short distance before landing out of the reach of the turning water. Zale had also landed close by and was bobbing up and down in the water as he recovered from the ordeal.

Both looking around for Raulf, of whom there was no sign.

Raulf approached the red pole which was the finish line. From here he could fly back to the platform on the beach and the challenge would be his to claim. Flaring his blue aura in excitement he whooped with joy.

Queen Shahmaran looked towards Zi, “This is not good Zi!”, she exclaimed quietly. Rebel will have to win the next three if he is to claim the Kingdom for Varick. Zi nodded, "I am disappointed Manasa, but have faith in Rebel".

Close by Yinshi, God of the Panthera looked down at the scene below, a look of admiration on his face. Rebel had surprised him, pleasantly so. He had not expected his grandson to forfeit the challenge for the life of a Felinia. As God of the Panthera, Yinshi also looked after the Felinia Clowder as they were of the same feline roots. Perhaps he was mistaken in his hatred of his daughter marrying into the Dragonians.

Yinshi watched as Raulf took flight towards the beach and the platforms, anger on his face, that Raulf would leave his partner Jonas to die such a death.

Raulf was ahead of Rebel and Zale by half a league and "no one was going to catch him", he thought to himself.

Rebel looked towards Zale as they flew towards the beach, both acknowledging each other and their attempts to help Jonas. As they approached their respective platforms, they could see Raulf walking towards the Dias, where his father King Varick was sitting.

Raulf had only a few supporters who cheered for him, but he did not care, he was one step closer to his dream of a Key, the Crown, and the Kingdom.

* * *

THE END

europe books